Dear Wade,

It is not conveni this time. There forward with eith ng in my last letter, aid you, despite your s on

I can be available for a court appearance if it's legally required. Otherwise, I will leave it to you and your lawyer to make the necessary arrangements.

Sincerely,

Joanna Lloyd ~~Hollister~~

Please address questions and book requests to: Harlequin Reader Service
U.S.: 3010 Walden Ave., P.O. Box 1325, Buffalo, NY 14269
Canadian: P.O. Box 609, Fort Erie, Ont. L2A 5X3

WESTERN *Lovers*™

SUSAN FOX

NOT PART OF THE BARGAIN

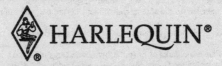

HARLEQUIN®

TORONTO • NEW YORK • LONDON
AMSTERDAM • PARIS • SYDNEY • HAMBURG
STOCKHOLM • ATHENS • TOKYO • MILAN • MADRID
PRAGUE • WARSAW • BUDAPEST • AUCKLAND

HARLEQUIN BOOKS
225 Duncan Mill Road, Don Mills,
Ontario, Canada M3B 3K9

ISBN 0-373-30195-2

NOT PART OF THE BARGAIN

This edition published by arrangement with Harlequin Books S.A.

® and TM are trademarks of the publisher. Trademarks indicated with
® are registered in the United States Patent and Trademark Office, the
Canadian Trade Marks Office and in other countries.

Visit us at www.eHarlequin.com

Printed in U.S.A.

CHAPTER ONE

WADE HOLLISTER inched the Buick around the corner, scanning house numbers while he tried to keep the rented vehicle from sliding on the snow- and ice-packed street. Huge snowflakes floated all around, limiting visibility to a half block and increasing his irritation.

He hadn't expected his plane to be slowed by the March snowstorm that had all but crippled the Midwest. He'd spent eighteen hours in St. Louis while he waited for the weather to break, then another six hours for the runways to be cleared and his flight number to be called. His plane had landed in Des Moines just as another late-winter storm blew in from Nebraska. Although he'd shaved and wangled a shower and a fresh change of clothes, Wade was in a foul temper and certainly in no mood to use the diplomacy he'd intended with Joanna.

Joanna. Just thinking of her deepened his bad mood. The letters he'd sent her these past three months had either gone unanswered, or elicited short, polite little refusals to return to Texas. But that was typical of her, he grumbled to himself, or of what little he knew of her. What he remembered was an artless, impossibly clumsy seventeen-year-old who rarely spoke, and hardly ever to him. His marrying Joanna hadn't changed that by much, since she'd disappeared three days after the wedding. But then, theirs had hardly been a conventional marriage.

Wade pulled the car into an icy parking slot and switched off the engine as he reached for his black Stetson. The brisk walk to the front door of the new-looking, two-story redwood-and-brick apartment building dispelled some of his tiredness but not his irritation. Before he stepped up to the main door, Wade cast a glance at the stately older homes nearby, his frown deepening as he noted the quaint, neatly kept neighborhood.

The people he'd hired to keep an eye on Joanna and send him periodic reports had indicated that, although she was currently unemployed, she had done all right for herself. Now that he could see for himself just how well she had done, he expected her to put up a much stronger resistance to moving back to Texas than he had anticipated. But that was just too bad, he decided. He didn't intend to take no for an answer.

JOANNA SAT on the floor near the furnace vent, busily searching the help-wanted ads for a secretarial position. It had been only a week since the furniture store she'd worked for had gone out of business, but she was worried her modest savings wouldn't last long enough for her to find something that paid reasonably well.

She could always give in and return to Texas, she reminded herself. But Joanna resisted that idea. The very thought of ever facing Wade Hollister again and putting herself under the control of a man who'd seen her as a necessary burden—and undoubtedly as an embarrassment—was as painful and offensive to her now as it had been three years before when she was almost eighteen.

Even her father had thought her little more than a nuisance back then—a problem he was all too eager to be rid of. A fresh swell of memory burst over her of what it had been like to finally be allowed to live with her father—only to have him leap at the chance to marry her off to a neighbor to cement a business agreement.

Lately those bitter memories, which she had thought she'd buried forever, had reawakened. In the most vivid of them she and Wade Hollister stood before a justice of the peace. The image was as sharp as the knife that had twisted in her seventeen-year-old heart when she'd realized that to Wade their marriage vows meant no more than fulfilling the unpleasant part of the cold financial agreement he'd made with her father.

Although she'd known that no man—particularly no man like Wade Hollister—would have given her so much as a second look back then if marriage to her hadn't given him access to a ranch and a small fortune, she'd still been cruelly disappointed by just how businesslike the arrangement really was. In the days between the agreement and the wedding, Wade had been as cold and emotionally distant toward her as her father had always been.

When her father suddenly suffered a stroke just two days before the wedding, Wade had softened toward her somewhat, but the running of both his ranch and her father's had taken up most of his time. She'd barely seen him until the wedding ceremony, but that hadn't kept her foolish heart from hoping for at least some sign from Wade that she wasn't quite the millstone around his neck that his indifference implied.

A few hours after the ceremony, her father had a second major stroke and died. Although Wade had been sympathetic, the wall of emotional and physical restraint between them had not been breached. She had learned since then to develop more realistic expectations.

Wade had been a desperate man three years ago. After his younger brother had virtually bankrupted the ranch that had been in the Hollister family for generations, Wade had been hesitant to approach local bankers, fearing a scandal should it become public knowledge that his brother, who'd since died, had signed over Hollister holdings to cover his bad investments and secret gambling debts.

Her father had seen Wade's misfortune as a timely opportunity. Joanna had been little more than a chattel in the agreement between the two men, which provided William Lloyd with a new way to push her out of his life, while it gave Wade discreet access to the money he needed.

Joanna's soft mouth turned down at the corners as

she thought again how eager her father had been to get rid of her and how desperate Wade must have been to marry her.

At least Wade hadn't suffered marriage to her for long. She'd fled Texas just after her father's funeral, in order to prove to Wade that she wanted him no more than he seemed to want her. Those first months had been hard, living on what she made from a string of jobs as a waitress while she tried to elude the private detectives Wade sent after her. But once she'd persuaded him to call off the detectives and leave her alone, she'd secured a small student loan and attended secretarial school for a year. She'd landed her first job with a small furniture store in Des Moines and had worked there until the declining Iowa economy took its toll on the small business.

Joanna had just finished marking a few job possibilities in the paper with a felt pen when she heard a sharp knock. She tossed the hurriedly folded paper onto the coffee table, got to her feet gracefully and started for the door. Thinking the paperboy was there to collect as usual on a Sunday afternoon, Joanna grabbed the yellow envelope off the counter that separated the kitchen from the dining area. The knock came again, louder this time, but she smiled, tolerant of the youngster's impatience as she unlocked the door and twisted the knob.

A gasp of surprise lodged in her throat as a shiny belt buckle caught the light, its elegantly scripted H winking at her from just below the place she had expected nine-year-old Bobby Smith's face to be. Panicked recognition sent her startled gaze higher.

From his lean, silver-buckled waist to his muscular chest and wide shoulders, Wade Hollister was the same towering, intimidating man of iron she remembered. But when her rounded hazel eyes reached his face, framed by thick black hair and wearing a stern expression, she easily detected the subtle difference three years had wrought.

Vivid blue eyes that had rarely paid her more than minimal attention were now riveted on her, their unwavering regard causing her own gaze to falter. She lowered her eyes to his harshly set, strongly defined mouth, then followed the firm line of his jaw, helpless to turn away from the rugged handsomeness that had only grown more appealing over the years.

"Joanna…?" Doubt was evident in the way Wade looked at her. Joanna was too taken by surprise to detect the glimmer of male interest that sparkled for the briefest moment in those vivid depths. The man she'd dreaded seeing again was standing before her, and color fled her cheeks as shock spread through her system.

Wade was experiencing a shock of his own as his hard stare took in everything about her slender, five-foot-four frame. He would have known those over-large, green-flecked brown eyes anywhere, and the unruly honey-streaked brown hair that couldn't make up its mind whether to be blond or brown. But the fact that Joanna had learned to make the most of the delicate, even features, which three years ago had promised beauty when she matured a little more, caught him off guard.

Though she wore almost no makeup and her shoulder-length, wavy curls were twisted into a loose knot at the back of her head, Joanna's transformation from an awkward adolescent into a poised young woman was total. Not even the faded jeans and oversize white blouse she had on detracted from her loveliness. Why the hell hadn't he been told?

"May I come in?"

Joanna's first impulse was to close the door. She hadn't realized she'd started to do just that until those intense blue eyes shifted to catch the slight movement, then returned to her face. He arched a brow in wordless reproach and Joanna stiffened.

"Why are you here?" To her surprise, she didn't retreat, but her challenge lacked any real assertiveness. If it was possible, she thought, Wade had a tougher, harder look about him than she remembered, and she fought against the irrational desire to shrink away and find a place to hide.

"We need to talk." The black Stetson Wade held in one hand began to rotate slightly on lean, impatient fingers.

Joanna hesitated a moment more, then stepped back, compelled as much by her innate sense of politeness as by Wade's impatience.

His entry into the apartment seemed to diminish her solitude by slow degrees, weakening her in some subtle way. Joanna watched Wade's back warily as she closed the door, deeply unnerved by his sudden intrusion into her life.

"I could use some coffee, if you have some," came the low, rough drawl as Wade turned from his quick survey of her home and looked directly at her. His sheepskin coat was still draped over his arm, his hat in hand, but Joanna was incapable of reaching out to take them.

Instead she stepped into the kitchen, grateful for an excuse to escape Wade's suffocating nearness and gather her wits. Today had been such an ordinary Sunday, quiet, uneventful, predictable. But now that Wade was here, the world had suddenly shifted on its axis. Joanna poured the last of the steaming coffee into two cups, amazed at the steadiness of her hands.

Wade had come to take her back to Texas. She knew that as certainly as she knew the sun rose in the morning. Although he'd never said as much in any of the letters he'd sent to persuade her to return, Joanna guessed now that she'd always known he would come after her eventually. Hadn't some secret part of her entertained the hope that he would? But the companion to that hope was the impossible fantasy that Wade was coming after her to give their mockery of a marriage a chance.

Joanna turned toward the large, open combination dining-living room, her gaze alighting on Wade's lean length before skittering away. *Don't kid yourself,* she cautioned silently. Wade's presence here was strictly business. The only fantasies and sappy emotions involved were her own.

He had thrown his coat over one arm of the sofa and upended the Stetson on a lamp table. The sheer size of the man seemed to dwarf everything she owned, from the powder-blue armchair and sofa to the large gray recliner in the corner. Nothing she possessed would accommodate that six-foot-four body to any degree of real comfort, she realized as she placed his coffee on the coffee table.

"All right if I sit down?" The not quite polite tone of his question indicated he wasn't in the best humor. She nodded, then felt faintly disturbed that her first impulse had been to appease him.

Joanna took her coffee and sat at the far corner of the sofa, unconsciously judging it the most secure place. She watched through her downswept lashes as Wade bent his imposing height, then settled in the armchair, one long leg stretched out at an angle that bypassed the coffee table and seemed to reach halfway across the room. Several unpleasant moments dragged by while he picked up his cup and drank, seeming to relax a little.

Joanna waited silently, scarcely moving, scarcely breathing, struck again, as she'd been in the past, by the impression that Wade Hollister was a man just like her father—distant, unfeeling and harsh. She was not aware that her carefully remote expression projected an annoying aloofness to her visitor. And he was in no mood to tolerate that aloofness. Instead her wordless reserve nettled him further.

"I want you to come back home with me," Wade began without preamble as he set his cup aside.

Joanna's eyes flew to his, seeing the determination on his unsmiling face, feeling the depth of it in the blue eyes that had darkened to the color of gunmetal.

"Texas was never home for me," she got out. "I don't belong there now any more than I did then."

"Belonging isn't the issue," Wade cut in. "You and I have business to settle." And from his tone of voice, there was no room for argument.

Joanna knew instantly that if she didn't speak up, Wade would walk right over her and disregard her wishes as heartlessly as they'd been disregarded before. It was that thought, that fear, that restored her courage.

"I indicated in my letters to you that I was agreeable to either annulment or divorce," she began slowly. "I thought I made it clear I would make no financial claims." Joanna assumed her inheritance no longer existed, long ago absorbed into Hollister interests. The agreement between Wade and her father had put Wade in charge of her father's ranch and financial assets to use as he saw fit. She seriously doubted that he had been able to hold on to the Double L, even if he had been able to save his Ten Star ranch. Probably neither he nor her father had been too concerned about whether she would have anything left to inherit. Joanna told herself she didn't care.

"It's not that simple." The impatience she'd sensed in him earlier had returned. "Your father and I had an agreement that included teaching you something about ranching so you could deal with a foreman when you took over the Double L."

Joanna shook her head slightly. "Is there anything left of the Double L?"

From the abrupt darkening of Wade's expression, Joanna realized she'd asked the worst possible question.

"I wouldn't be here if I'd failed," he told her, his low voice just above a growl.

Of course not, she answered silently as she read the steady confidence in his strong, proud face, the iron will and determination to succeed that rested as naturally on those broad shoulders as snowfall on the mountains. From the top of his head to the bottom of his underslung heels, Wade was the epitome of everyone's romantic notion of the successful Texan. He not only looked the part of the understated millionaire rancher, he had evidently achieved it for himself.

"I'm not interested in the Double L," she said at last. "As far as I'm concerned, your agreement with my father had nothing to do with my someday taking over his ranch. He wanted to lend you money, and he wanted to find someplace else to send me. You got your money, and I took care of the burden to you by leaving." She spoke matter-of-factly, as if being pressured into marriage with a reluctant stranger who'd married her solely to get his hands on her father's money was not the hurt it really was.

Wade's gaze narrowed suddenly. Joanna forced herself to maintain eye contact with the perceptive look he was giving her.

"The Double L is yours," he pointed out then, his voice a bit gruffer. "And now that I'm ready to turn over the running of it to you, it's time you came home and took over your responsibilities.''

''I have a life here,'' she insisted firmly, uncomfortable with the new pressure Wade was bringing to bear. But Wade merely smiled, a skeptical quirk of lips that easily dismissed her objection.

''And I have a prior claim on that life, Joanna.'' The low words slid like velvet across her emotions. ''Legally you're still my wife.''

Joanna stared at the cold glimmer in those vivid blue eyes, a contradiction to the possessiveness so distinct in his deep rich drawl.

''I'm certain that means as little to you as it does to me,'' she rallied frostily, then looked away and sipped her coffee—anything to break away from that penetrating regard.

''Nevertheless I gave my word to your father. I need you to come back to Texas so I can keep that word.'' Wade was immovable.

Joanna set down her cup in frustration and got to her feet. The roomy one-bedroom apartment, which had seemed more than large enough for her, was suddenly too small, too stuffy. Wade was overwhelming her privacy with his presence, disrupting it with the demands he was making of her. She was accustomed to shutting out the rest of the world once she was on the inside of her apartment door. Rarely did she allow anyone to violate the solitude that had become her habit. Now, not only was it being violated, this man was insisting she give it up.

''Since my father seldom allowed me to live with

him, I know nothing about ranching," she reminded him, pacing toward the sliding glass doors that looked out on a snow-drifted balcony. "Wouldn't it be simpler to just sell the Double L?" Her relief at hitting upon a reasonable solution evaporated quickly.

"Simpler, yes," Wade agreed harshly. "But if you recall, your father's will makes the stipulation that you can't sell out for at least two years after I hand the property over to you."

Joanna flung a look over her shoulder at the big rancher who was watching her so closely. There was a sharpness in his gaze now, almost a rebuke.

"And, I can hand it over to you only after I teach you enough to run it with the help of a foreman," he went on.

Joanna looked scornful. "I'll bet you're looking forward to that."

"It was part of the deal I agreed to," he said coolly.

Joanna looked away, resenting Wade's sense of responsibility, yet hating her father's lack of it as a parent.

"Your father wanted you to have the Double L, Joanna," Wade continued when she kept silent, "and since he worked most of his life to build it up, he wanted you to care as much for it as he did. You wouldn't do that if you could just sell out and walk away. Learning how to run the Double L and living there for a couple of years might give you the time you need."

Her lips curled faintly. "I tried living there once," she said softly, thinking back to that time....

The cranky, strict old-maid aunt her father had sent her to live with when she was five years old, had died just after she turned sixteen, and Joanna had refused to stay in the private school he sent her to next. She still remembered the day she'd shown up at the Double L, barely one week into the school term, bags in hand, determined to stay. The explosive display of temper she'd expected didn't come, but she ended up suffering her father's silence and apparent indifference toward her for months after he at last granted permission for her to stay.

When William Lloyd learned of Wade's financial problems, he'd discovered another, more permanent way of pushing his only child out of his life, and he'd grabbed at the chance. Those memories were etched indelibly in Joanna's mind, along with the ongoing sense of being unloved and unwanted that she feared she'd carry for the rest of her life.

"Well?"

Joanna felt herself go slack. Wade had told her after her father died that he'd handle everything to do with the Double L until he got things straightened out. He'd made it clear then, as her father's will had made it clear, that she was to take it over one day. When Wade's letters had started coming, she'd been forced to acknowledge to herself that even if the ranch hadn't survived, the marriage she'd fled three years before was still waiting for her, still preventing her from establishing anything permanent somewhere else.

Despite Wade's unwelcome arrival now, she felt a measure of relief that he had managed to keep the Double L for her after all, and that this last bit of unfinished business concerning their marriage and his agreement with her father was about to be resolved. Besides, her roots were in Texas. Though she hadn't got to spend much time there after her mother's death, she'd always wanted to live on the ranch. She still had a few golden memories of how happy she'd been while her mother was alive.

Her father had been different, then, too. She'd never understood why he suddenly changed toward her and sent her away, never understood the reason behind his constant efforts to keep her away from her home. William Lloyd's repeated rejection had affected her deeply, inflicting wounds on a stunned and grief-stricken five-year-old that had never quite healed, yet had never quite destroyed her love for him.

She had to go back to Texas and live at the ranch, she realized, especially now that she knew the Double L was still hers. In spite of her confused feelings about her father, deep down she still wanted to have some part of him, even if all it amounted to was the ranch he'd worked most of his life to build up. It was some consolation to her pride that Wade had come to her, that she hadn't been forced to go back to Texas because she'd not been able to make it on her own. She'd done all right alone, and after an apprenticeship of sorts with Wade she might be able to continue to do so, though on a much larger scale.

"When would you like me to go back?" she asked, absently watching the snow swirls beyond the huge sheets of glass, her mind already beginning to make plans.

"I have two plane tickets for tomorrow at five in the afternoon," came the low voice.

Dismayed, Joanna shook her head. "That's too soon."

"It's not soon enough, Joanna," Wade returned. "And since you've just joined the ranks of the unemployed, there's no reason for you to put it off."

Joanna turned to face him. "How did you know?"

Wade's gaze was remote. "You don't think I'd allow a teenage girl I was responsible for live on her own completely unsupervised, do you?"

Joanna stared, her lips parting in fresh surprise. "You had someone spy on me? All this time? I thought I'd put a stop to that." She hadn't even suspected! Wade had promised to call off the private detectives he'd sent after her, and she'd assumed that was the end of it.

"Someone's kept track of you since the day I agreed to let you spend some time on your own," he admitted, clearly unconcerned by the first glimmers of resentment in her hazel eyes. "If you'd had any problems or got into any trouble, you would have been back on the Ten Star before the dust could settle."

Outrage brought a full flush to her cheeks. "I doubt that."

Several moments of silence enveloped them, the discordant currents in the room fairly crackling between them. At just the moment Joanna vowed she'd never return to Texas with this arrogant, manipulative man, he expelled a long weary breath, his stern manner easing.

"I'm sorry if that riles you, Joanna. Hiring someone to watch over you here was the only way I could figure to let you have your way and still be able to sleep nights. Having me look out for your interests was one of the few things you got out of this lopsided deal, and I meant to do a good job of it."

Joanna realized instantly that he wasn't apologizing for hiring people to watch over her; he'd merely said he was sorry his actions riled her. It was his mention of the "lopsided deal" that hinted at genuine apology, and Joanna found his confession mildly disarming.

"Just like I mean to do a good job of fulfilling the final part of the agreement," he went on, the utter seriousness on his face muting her resistance. "This is a busy time of year for me, Joanna—for us. I've already tried coaxing you home," he said, reminding her of the letters he'd already sent, "but time's running out."

Joanna turned back to the window, feeling uncomfortably restless as her desire to finally have something of her father's warred against her unwillingness to allow Wade to uproot her so abruptly. In little more than twenty-four hours he expected her just to pack a bag and get on a plane with him.

"What about my furniture, my plants?" she asked, softening, knowing it wasn't reasonable to resist Wade too strenuously when she'd already decided to return to Texas.

"I've got movers coming in by two tomorrow to take care of everything. All you need to do is inventory your things."

Joanna's shoulders went rigid. "You're very sure of yourself," she said, wishing now she hadn't signaled her acquiescence quite so soon.

"I was determined."

A light shiver ran over her skin at the words, but she gave no outward sign of it as she turned to face him.

Wade had slumped in the armchair, his lean fingers linked together and resting on his middle, his long legs stretched out in front of him. He was the picture of relaxation, his eyes half-closed with evident self-satisfaction now that he'd got what he wanted. Joanna bristled.

"Which hotel are you staying at?" Since she'd more or less agreed to return to Texas, she was eager for Wade to leave so she could recover her composure in privacy and get organized. Her question was a not so subtle invitation for him to take himself elsewhere.

"I was figuring on staying here tonight."

Joanna tilted her head slightly, thinking she hadn't heard correctly. Wade's lips twisted as her face registered understanding.

"But I don't have room for you." She glanced toward the short hallway that led to the only bedroom.

"I'll take the sofa," he said, his eyes twinkling lazily, obviously finding something about the situation amusing.

"That's not possible," she argued, realizing belatedly the importance of meeting Wade's every aggression with equal resistance.

"I can fall asleep anywhere, Joanna. Don't worry about me." Wade's eyes closed, but his lips eased into a half grin as he deliberately misunderstood her concern.

"You can't stay here," Joanna said firmly. "It's not…proper."

"We're husband and wife."

"But we aren't," she insisted and Wade's eyes opened fractionally. "Not really, we aren't," she corrected, her face stung with color.

His gaze ran over her assessingly. "That's true enough," he admitted. "But what about the storm?"

Joanna glanced toward the glass doors, realizing with some chagrin that the storm was likely the sole reason he was planning to stay, not because he might have any belated designs on her virtue.

"It should let up soon," she offered quickly, hoping that the forecast of more snow mixed with freezing rain was wrong. "You should be able to get to a motel after the snowplows come by."

Wade's lips formed a skeptical line. "And if they don't?"

She laced her fingers together uneasily. "That

would be different, of course,'' she conceded. ''Perhaps if you were to leave right now—'' Joanna broke off when she heard the tinkle of sleet hitting the huge panes of glass.

The snow seemed to have abated slightly, but only enough for a little freezing rain to add a treacherous layer of ice to the already hazardous conditions outside. As she stood breathlessly and listened, the tiny bits of ice hitting the glass seemed to intensify.

''I need to catch a few minutes' sleep.'' Wade's voice drew her attention back to his face. ''Unless you'd rather I took my chances outside.''

Joanna glanced hopefully toward the windows, then reluctantly shook her head, forced to concede that Wade should stay—at least until the snowplows came by or the city sent out sand and salt trucks.

''Would you wake me in about an hour?''

Joanna murmured a response, but Wade's eyes had closed. She watched, suspicious at first, then slightly amazed as she detected the change in his breathing and realized he had fallen asleep almost instantly. It was then she noticed the tired lines at his mouth, the fatigue that made his jaw go slack. After staring at him a bit longer, she picked up their coffee cups and carried them into the kitchen.

For supper she decided to reheat the vegetable stew and serve it with the crusty bread she'd baked the day before. There would be plenty for two. Another quick look at Wade told her he was sleeping deeply, the harshness of his face gone soft, giving his rugged handsomeness an even deeper kind of appeal.

Although she was beginning to relax, Joanna felt bruised inside, jolted by Wade's sudden appearance and his demand that she return to Texas. Yet there was also a growing sense of calm, a deep-down sense of peace that told her she'd been right to give in without too much fuss.

But that peace scattered the moment she stepped into her bedroom and switched on the light, reminded by the sight of the bed of Wade's intention to stay the night. Knowing he'd stated a preference for the sofa gave her little comfort, and Joanna quietly closed the door, then leaned back against it, the details of her room blurring.

This apartment had been her home, one of the few places in her life where she felt entirely welcome, protected by the solitude she'd learned to retreat into as a child. A trembling began deep inside as old hurts and insecurities began to stir and swell, cruel reminders of the painful, life-shaping rejections she had known. She closed her eyes as the horrible sense of being unwanted threatened to return to haunt and overwhelm.

Joanna thought she now understood why it was so important for her to return to Texas with Wade, and so imperative that their departure be tomorrow. "He's finally divorcing me," she whispered to herself. Although she'd always known he would someday, the certainty of knowing Wade would soon divorce her hurt in a way she hadn't expected.

Joanna chided herself for the feeling. This was not personal, she reminded herself. She and Wade didn't even know each other. It wasn't as if she was a failure at being a wife. Heavens, she didn't even have a wedding ring!

But as she stood, leaning back against that smooth, hard door, Joanna suddenly found herself wondering what it would be like to be loved by a man like Wade, to be part of a family and have children of her own. What would it be like to see that tough, handsome face soften with love for her, or to have those strong arms reach for her in the night?

Joanna thrust herself from the door and paced to the window.

What a dreamer she was, what a fool! Her own father hadn't wanted her; he'd never been able to tolerate having her around. His rejection had left her with little faith in blood ties and almost none in emotional relationships of any kind. If blood couldn't bind soul to soul, vows couldn't, either. She had learned to be self-sufficient, to count on no one but herself, and she didn't need anyone, least of all Wade Hollister.

But how many more years could she live in the emotional void she'd endured most of her life? Joanna was weary of solitude and infrequent, shallow friendships.

There was a reservoir of love inside her that churned against the dam of emotional restraint fear had erected. Although outwardly she grew more and more poised, more and more aloof, the barriers inside were slowly being eroded, like the wasting abrasion of a river against a riverbank as it sought to alter its course. Joanna knew herself well enough to sense that she was precariously close to the day when either the dam would burst, or the persistent action of the river would divert itself into a new channel.

Whichever it might be—the bursting of the dam or the quiet shift and overflow of the river—Joanna prayed Wade Hollister would not be the one who stood in the path of the flood.

CHAPTER TWO

THE NEXT DAY passed in a blur of activity. The streets had been sanded and salted before the morning rush hour, enabling Wade to drive Joanna around town in order to pay her bills and close her bank accounts. Just after lunch they began an inventory of her belongings for the movers. Their late-afternoon flight took them to Dallas/Fort Worth, where they made the necessary connections to San Antonio. By then it was late evening, and Joanna collapsed gratefully into her bed at their hotel.

The day that followed was equally busy.

"I made up a list of the things you're going to need at the ranch," Wade told her at breakfast as he pulled a piece of paper from his shirt pocket and thrust it in her direction. "I figured we'd spend the day shopping and fly home tomorrow."

Wade sipped his coffee while Joanna's eyes passed quickly over the bold handwriting, out of habit translating the list into dollars and cents. The total would severely deplete her small savings. Then, as if he'd read her mind, Wade told her, "I'll worry about the cost."

"Will I really need all these things?" She could

understand the need for many of the items on the list, such as boots, Stetson, jeans and other outdoor clothing. But it was the quantity that gave her pause, as well as the inclusion of spurs, chaps and gloves she assumed only Wade and their ranch hands had need of.

"I can't teach you much about ranching until you see how things work," he explained to her, his calming drawl an unspoken assurance that he was prepared to be patient with her. "The best way to understand the work and the people who will be working for you is to have a taste of the life and work yourself." Wade leaned back then, his blue gaze mildly appraising. "And you'd better think about buying some dresses and such if you don't already have plenty. Spring and summer usually bring a few get-togethers you'll want to go to so you can meet your neighbors." A look of discomfort flickered in his eyes for the briefest moment before he hastily added, "It may be weeks before we're back where shopping's this good."

Later, Wade drove them literally from one end of town to the other, determined to buy everything on the list and have it stowed in the trunk of their rental car before the end of the day. But by the time they returned to their hotel for dinner that evening, the easier, friendlier moments they'd had at breakfast had deteriorated into silence, the brittle formality between them broken only by a few laconic words from Wade whenever a nod or a gesture would not communicate what he had in mind.

Joanna might have felt in tune with Wade's silence

had it been motivated by a quiet reserve like her own. But it wasn't, she was slowly realizing, more certain by the moment that Wade was regretting now that he'd brought her back to Texas.

"WOULD YOU HAND ME that smaller case, Joanna?"

Joanna passed Wade the piece of luggage, watching as he loaded their purchases into the Cessna aircraft, struck by how compellingly handsome he was with his lips curved into a slight smile and his blue eyes almost jewellike with what was unmistakably anticipation. It occurred to her that he seemed especially pleased to be going home to the Ten Star. Or perhaps it wasn't just that. Did he have someone there he was eager to see?

Joanna glanced away and tugged the collar of her new down vest higher against the cool breeze. Of course. It had been three years, and Joanna wasn't fool enough to think that their pitiful little marriage of convenience had prevented Wade from looking elsewhere for the things he'd never wanted from her. She had no idea if many people even knew about their marriage, since it had been so secretive at the time. After she'd run away, Wade had likely gone on living just as he always had, and it was conceivable that he now had a serious relationship with someone, perhaps even someone he wanted to marry.

"Ready?"

Joanna nodded, then accepted the supporting hand Wade held out to help her step up into the plane. Once they were both seated in the small aircraft, she waited self-consciously as Wade carefully strapped her in, not understanding why his brisk, impersonal touch was sending a hundred shivering sensations through her.

Wade paused, his glance meeting hers. "Something wrong?"

Joanna blushed and shook her head. He studied the guilty traces of color in her cheeks and gave the belt a final tug before his long fingers released it.

He knew. Joanna nearly choked on her next breath. He knew he was having an effect on her. She looked away, her rigid profile a prim denial of what he had somehow guessed.

"Are you having second thoughts about coming back with me, or are you just nervous about this plane?" Wade asked after he finished with his pre-flight checklist and started the engine.

Joanna glanced over at him, catching the measuring look he was giving her. She shrugged, trying to feign nonchalance, but Wade's eyes narrowed, prompting her to answer. "Both."

One corner of Wade's mouth edged upward, and she felt the tension between them ease.

"All you have to remember about flying with me is that I want to avoid a plane crash as much as you do," he said as he reached for his sunglasses and slipped them on. "I'm sorry about the other," he told her, his lips slanting, "but it can't be helped." Then he turned back to the controls, his radio headset in place as he conversed with the control tower and the Cessna began to taxi toward a runway.

Joanna looked out her window, already knowing that Wade considered himself honor bound to fulfill his agreement with her father. It was becoming quite clear to her that no matter how either of them felt about it, Wade was determined to hold them both to the bargain.

The flight wasn't a long one, and soon Wade was telling Joanna to watch for the ranch below. "Your father left you a damned good piece of Texas, Joanna," he added, glancing over at her only long enough to catch her nod of agreement.

Joanna watched with interest as Wade flew the small plane over the Double L, pointing out landmarks. The Double L, like his Ten Star, was situated southwest of Ozona, Texas. Founded on miles of rolling prairie, both ranches were on prime land on the semiarid Stockton Plateau, with the Ten Star sprawling over parts of three counties. Yet everything Wade told her was intended as a refresher of what he assumed she already knew.

So she remained silent, not attempting to correct his misconception. She didn't quite know how to tell him that, in the almost two years she'd lived with her father, she had seen no more of the Double L than could be viewed from a ranch road or the house.

After the failure of her attempt to ride a horse for the first time, her father hadn't urged her to try again, and Joanna had figured he could tell that she'd never be a good-enough rider for him to bother with. She had been virtually housebound after that, and though she occasionally went down to the barns to pet a few of the new foals, she'd never managed to gather enough courage to insist that her father again try to teach her to ride so she could be part of his life. Nearly two years later the fact that he'd left everything he owned to her, and indicated in his will that he wanted her to someday run the ranch, had been a genuine surprise.

"You'll be staying at the Ten Star," Wade was saying to her now. She turned her head sharply, thinking she hadn't heard correctly. "It'll be easier for you to learn and easier for me if we don't have to waste time getting together," he explained before he banked the aircraft and headed it toward the Ten Star.

The Hollister Ten Star was one of the largest ranches in southwest Texas, its 200,000-plus acres dwarfing the smaller Double L.

"We struck oil nearly a year ago," Wade told her over the steady hum of the engine as they flew over the high, flat expanse of range now dotted with a handful of pumping rigs that drew the ancient fossil fuel from deep in the earth.

Joanna leaned toward her window to glance obligingly at the wells below, secretly resenting the fact the bottoming out of the oil industry four years ago had prevented Wade from drilling in time to recoup his losses, thereby making their marriage necessary. She realized with some surprise that she also resented that he had now found oil in abundance enough to secure his freedom from her. Oil would have replenished the drained resources of the Ten Star much more easily than the arrangement with Joanna's father, but Wade felt he had no other choice at the time; on top of which, his late father had never wanted to mar the beauty of the Ten Star, when the Hollisters made a comfortable-enough living by ranching and careful vigilance over their investments.

She glanced over at Wade wondering if he'd agonized much over his decision to drill for oil. But that was something she'd probably never be privy to, keeping in mind that they would soon be going their separate ways. At best theirs would be little more than a business relationship, not reason enough for either of them to share much of their lives beyond what was necessary.

Joanna forced her attention to the scattering of clay-red Santa Gertrudis cattle strung across the Ten Star range below, catching an occasional glimpse of a mounted cowhand. According to Wade, the calf crop had been good on both ranches this year, in spite of the fact, he added with a wry twist, that beef prices were down. Joanna didn't need to be told that oil production on the Ten Star would more than make up for the high-cost, high-risk proposition that ranching was nowadays.

It was only a few minutes later that the small plane began its descent. The main buildings of the Ten Star were surrounded and overhung by trees whose branches were already covered with spring leaves and some with bright blossoms. Tall barns sat among a huge network of corrals placed a comfortable distance from a large bunkhouse and several smaller houses, which were clearly one-family dwellings.

But nothing quite prepared her for the sight of the two-story wood-and-stone ranch house with its red-tile roof. The large structure boasted adobe archways along the front and a stone patio at the back surrounding a tarp-covered swimming pool. Joanna caught a brief glimpse of a second-story balcony with wrought-iron railings and an outside staircase to the patio, before the wing of the aircraft obstructed her view.

As the plane finished its circle and began to drop quickly to the landing strip a half mile from the main house, Joanna tried to deal with her shock over the obvious wealth a home like that indicated. The house on the Double L was a simple one, and though large, it possessed none of the character and opulence of Wade's home.

For the first time, Joanna wondered how in the world Wade and her father had expected the modest resources of the Double L to help replenish, on such an enormous scale, those of the Ten Star. The small craft taxied to a stop in front of a hangar before she could give voice to her surprise.

"This isn't what I expected," she finally said as she watched Wade remove his sunglasses and unbuckle his seat belt.

"What isn't?" he asked distractedly while he scanned the controls one last time and made a few notations in a flight log.

"Your home," she clarified as she unfastened her own seat belt. "It's…quite grand."

Wade didn't spare her so much as a glance.

"You've seen it before," he said, leaning past her to lever open her door.

"No, I haven't." Her quiet disagreement caused a moment's hesitation before those vividly blue eyes connected with hers.

"Sure you have."

Joanna shook her head. "You never brought me here," she reminded him firmly, her face suddenly flushed with an unintentional spurt of temper at his doubtful look. "I always thought you were too ashamed of me to bring me here."

Joanna turned and climbed out of the plane, astonished at herself and the bitterness deep inside that had spilled past her reserve. More astonishing was the fact that instead of feeling apprehensive about angering Wade she felt an oddly satisfying sense of release.

The slender, dark-haired figure that ran toward them from where a pickup truck was parked kept Wade and Joanna from speaking again. "Welcome to the Ten Star!"

The moment Joanna saw Megan Hollister, she knew who she was. Tall, model-slim, her aura of self-confidence bordering on arrogance, Megan was the same age as Joanna—twenty-one—and, if it were possible, the green-eyed brunette was even more beautiful than she'd been in high school.

Warily Joanna reached out for the eager handshake Wade's sister was offering, taken aback by the welcome. But then, in the two years they'd gone to the same school, Megan had rarely seemed to notice

Joanna existed, so it was entirely possible Megan didn't recognize her.

"So—" Megan released her hand and grinned up at Wade "—you couldn't get Joanna to come back with you, huh?" The laughter in those deep green eyes was suddenly so like the humor Joanna had seen so often in school that she cringed. Megan's inclination to speak her mind and to make jokes at the expense of others had sometimes bordered on cruelty, and Joanna fervently hoped Megan had outgrown the tendency.

"This *is* Joanna." Wade's statement banished the amusement from his sister's face as her green eyes swung back to Joanna and traveled over her with disbelief. It was a long moment before the other woman seemed to recognize her, and when she did, her earlier welcoming attitude faded to marginally rude disinterest.

"Spanish Lady is in labor," Megan told her brother. "She's close."

Wade hesitated only a moment before he started for the pickup parked at the edge of the runway. Joanna stood, feeling awkward and uncertain whether to follow Wade or stay and unload her things from the plane, until an impatient gesture from him sent her rushing toward the pickup.

"Still the little shrinking violet, I see," Megan murmured challengingly as Joanna brushed past her.

But Joanna said nothing, giving no hint she'd even heard the remark as she slid to the middle of the bench seat to give Megan room to get in beside her.

Fifteen minutes later, Joanna stood outside the huge square stall, her rounded eyes shifting from Spanish Lady's shiny black hindquarters, to the frown of concentration on her husband's face. The tension inside the stall was heavy, yet almost electric as Wade checked the progress of the unborn foal.

Just moments ago, only one tiny hoof had presented itself, prompting Wade to scrub up quickly as he and Megan discussed the probability that the other hoof was caught on the rim of the mare's pelvis and had likely been deflected back into her uterus.

"Easy girl," Megan crooned softly as she grasped the mare's halter. Spanish Lady, damp with sweat and trembling nervously as she lay on the straw, accepted the invasion of her womb for only a few moments before she began to shift restlessly, flinging out a sturdy hoof as if to strike as Wade gently pressed the foal back toward the uterus to gain more room while he searched for the missing hoof.

Then he seemed to find what he was after, and murmuring to calm the young mare, he braced his free hand more firmly against the horse's rump. Slowly, his face growing flushed with the effort, he pulled the small hoof toward the birth canal taking care not to let it tear the wall of the uterus. At last he pulled his hand free.

Joanna could only stare, guessing from the fact that Wade and Megan were now leaving the stall that Wade had succeeded. In the next second, the mare lowered her quivering head to the thick bed of straw just in time for a new contraction to seize her.

"That should do it," Wade remarked in a subdued voice as he stepped out of the stall to the bucket of fresh water on a bench nearby. Keeping out of the way, Joanna watched as he cleaned up.

"Is she green around the gills yet?" Megan asked her brother as she followed him out and closed the stall's half door. The mocking smile on Megan's mouth was for Joanna.

Wade's head came up, and as he reached for the towel on the bench, he quickly scanned Joanna's face. "Do you have a weak stomach?" he asked her.

Joanna shook her head. "Not that I know of."

"Good." Wade tossed down the towel and joined his sister, the pair of them leaning companionably on the side of the stall, elbows resting on the top rail as they watched the mare and discussed her quickening progress.

Joanna might not have been there at all, she thought a bit resentfully before she reminded herself that Spanish Lady had clearly been having problems delivering her first foal. Suddenly it seemed churlish to expect Wade to take time out from what had nearly developed into a crisis in order to include her or to explain more than a few words about what was going on. Surely he would make time for her questions later.

Joanna stepped to the other side of Wade, peering over the top rail of the large stall, caught up in the mare's fear and excitement as the animal shifted on her bed of straw and whickered nervously.

The unhurried tread of a pair of boots coming down the wide stable aisle drew Joanna's attention briefly, then claimed it totally as a tall, lean cowboy ambled up, his dark eyes intent upon her face.

"Afternoon, Mrs. Hollister." The low drawl was as slow as molasses and brought a shy smile to Joanna's soft mouth as the cowboy touched a finger to the brim of his battered brown Stetson.

"Hello, Mr. Terrell."

"Jake," the big man insisted as he extended a tanned hand. Joanna hesitated only a moment before placing her fingers in his thickly callused palm. "You've grown up some," Jake remarked, his handsome face smiling, his expression warm.

Joanna shrugged slightly, then relaxed, feeling instantly at ease. Though he was Wade's age or a little younger, Jake Terrell had been a friend of her father's, and one of the few people who'd gone out of their way to pay her some attention during that isolated, lonely time she'd lived at the Double L.

Not that she'd seen Jake all that much, since he'd rarely come up to the house, but whenever he did join them for a meal, Jake had always managed to put her at ease, effortlessly coaxing her from her shy reserve. She would always be grateful for the sensitivity he'd shown toward an awkward adolescent who couldn't seem to make friends easily.

"It's good to see you," Joanna told him quietly, meaning it sincerely.

The handshake that should have been brief was not. Instead the warm pressure of Jake's lean fingers increased slightly as he smiled down at her. There was a spark of something different in that smile, and an even more curious glimmer in Jake's dark eyes that threw her for a moment. Confused, Joanna looked away, then she tugged her fingers from his grip.

"What brings you by, Jake?" Wade interjected, and Joanna sensed a small bit of harshness in his tone.

"I'll bet he's come by to invite me to the Brewsters' square dance Saturday night," Megan piped up as she stepped over to Jake and linked her arm with his.

Jake glanced down at the brunette beauty indulgently for a moment before he answered Wade. "Just wanted to stop over and welcome Joanna home," Jake answered as his eyes touched Joanna's. "Besides—" now his twinkling brown gaze shifted back to Megan "—seems to me you turned me down for that dance." Jake's slow Texas drawl was at once teasing and faintly scolding.

"I only turned you down because I was angry," Megan reminded him.

Joanna edged away from the pair, not comfortable standing in the middle of what was becoming an intimate conversation. However, the spot she'd chosen so she could see the mare wasn't much more comfortable, as now she was standing beside Wade. A quick sideways glance caught his unsmiling regard.

"Will I be in the way here?" she asked softly, sensing that anything above a whisper might alarm the mare.

"I'll let you know if you are," he answered, his voice almost a growl as he faced forward and watched the laboring mare inside the stall. Joanna watched, too, feeling compassion for the animal, who hovered between pain and restlessness. She attributed Wade's surliness to concern for the young horse.

"How much longer?" she whispered to him, noting with excitement that long slim forelegs and a dark muzzle, then a small, well-shaped head were presenting themselves.

All eyes as she witnessed the foal's birth, Joanna was unaware of Wade's close study of her gentle profile and the softening of his expression as he murmured, "Not long now."

And it wasn't more than a few moments until the neck and shoulders of the small creature emerged, followed quickly by the rest of its membrane-covered body. Joanna held her breath as the mare turned her head and stretched her neck toward the newborn.

A soft sigh of adoration escaped Joanna as the tiny damp body that seemed all legs struggled shakily on the straw, rending the rest of the filmy sac that still clung to it. In a remarkably short time, the foal worked itself free of the tissue and was lying almost beside its mother.

"He's so active," she whispered excitedly to Wade. "Shouldn't you cut the umbilical cord before he breaks it?"

"It's supposed to rupture on its own when *she* gets to *her* feet." Though he might have been impatient with her ignorance, there was only amusement in Wade's voice. Relieved yet chagrined, Joanna looked more closely at the newborn's sex, for the foal was now in a better position for her to see.

"I guess I wasn't looking," she murmured apologetically as she glanced sideways at Wade. She caught the half smile that lingered on his mouth, and she looked away, feeling the awe and excitement of the last half hour deepen.

A few minutes later, the gray foal with black stockings struggled to gain her footing in the straw. Knees buckling and balance wavering, the determined foal followed her instincts, finally, precariously, managing to stand on all four spindly legs. Spanish Lady had got to her feet by then herself, and soon the hungry youngster was butting her nose against her mother's leg, then her flank before she found what she was after and had a first taste of her mother's milk.

Emotion surged into Joanna's throat at the sight of Spanish Lady nudging her young one, whuffling softly, taking to mothering her first foal as if she'd done it many times before. The unexpected tenderness of the scene struck something deep inside Joanna, touching a yearning she'd never allowed herself to dwell on. How strange that now, in this unlikely place, in this stable that smelled strongly of horse and leather and hay, the longing to have a child was suddenly overwhelming.

As if her thoughts had somehow materialized in the air and given her away, Joanna glanced covertly at the other three people who had witnessed the foal's birth, astonished to see that their faces revealed none of the intense emotion she was feeling. But then, she had to remember that all of them had witnessed the birth of a foal countless times, whereas this had been her first. Yes, that must be why she was feeling so sentimental, she decided, choosing to ignore the thought that she was lying to herself.

"SPANISH LADY is a beautiful animal," Joanna began cautiously as she and Wade walked the half mile from the barn to the ranch house shortly before sunset. "What breed is she?"

"Arabian."

Joanna paused, trying to gauge from his terse answer whether he welcomed her curiosity or not. Few people in her growing-up years had had time for her questions, her cranky aunt and her father in particular. Then again, she was here to learn, and she had to assume that meant she was expected to ask questions, even if she had been at the Ten Star for just over three hours.

"I thought only quarter horses were used for ranch work. That was the kind my father used," she went on, hoping to get Wade to take over the conversation.

"I reckon mostly they are," he replied, his eyes meeting the serious intensity of hers. "But I'll use anything with cow sense. Nearly all the Arabians we own are used for pleasure riding, though we keep a few of them for working cattle." Wade smiled at her then, and Joanna felt her lips curve in an answering smile. For a few breathless moments they stared at each other, Wade shortening his long stride to match hers. "Will didn't let you go down to the barns when the mares were foaling, did he?"

Joanna's gaze shot away from his, a light flush touching her cheeks as she shook her head.

"I'm not surprised. He was probably afraid you'd ask him something he wouldn't be able to bring himself to explain," Wade said, then chuckled. "Springtime with a teenage girl on the place must have worn pretty hard on the old man's nerves."

Joanna didn't know what to say to that. She'd guessed her father was often uncomfortable with her, but she'd rarely been able to discern any reason other than he didn't really want her around. It hadn't occurred to her that his discomfort and lack of communication might have had something to do with an inability to deal with her, rather than mere dislike. It was a new thought, and one that took her attention as they passed the bunkhouse and the lane that led to five small single-family houses. She didn't speak again until they reached the stone patio of the huge ranch house.

"We forgot to get our things from the plane," Joanna reminded Wade as he opened the door just off the kitchen and escorted her into a large open room filled with the rich, meaty smell of broiled steak.

"It's already been taken care of," he replied as he scuffed his boots on the floor mat and hung his hat on a wooden peg next to the door. Joanna had just started to shrug out of her down vest when Wade reached over to assist her.

"I can get it," she said hastily, but couldn't pull back quickly enough to elude the strong fingers that caught her vest and tangled in a skein of honey-streaked hair. The gentle tug that resulted sent lightning streaks of sensation from her scalp to the depth of her being, and Joanna flushed guiltily, flustered by her strong reaction to the most casual physical contact with Wade.

"Just a minute," Wade murmured, his breath gusting over her cheek, her step away halted by his hold on that lock of hair. It seemed to Joanna that he took more time than necessary to release her. "I'm sorry. Did that hurt?"

"No." Joanna finally managed to distance herself from him, combing slim fingers through the silken curls that cascaded around her head to restore some order, but more to comb away the tingling sensations that still lingered. She couldn't look at him.

"Ah, there you are, Señor Hollister." An attractive middle-aged Mexican woman swept into the kitchen, the full hem of her gathered skirt swirling around thick ankles. Her wide white-toothed smile and sparkling black eyes were welcoming and respectful toward her employer, and Joanna sensed instantly the affection in her manner. "How was your trip?" the woman asked.

"Successful, Consuelo."

"Ah, good," Consuelo replied. "Dinner will be served when you are ready." Then the sparkling dark eyes turned to Joanna, the wide smile easing to a polite curve.

"Consuelo, this is my wife, Joanna," Wade began, and Joanna noticed he'd hesitated fractionally over the words *my wife*. And to Joanna, "This is our cook and housekeeper, Consuelo Garcia."

"Welcome to the Ten Star, Señora Hollister," Consuelo said, her black eyes turning serious. "I hope you will enjoy your stay with us."

Joanna nodded and murmured a quiet thank-you. Experience had taught her that few people ever took to her on sight, so Consuelo's almost stern welcome caused her little more than mild discomfort.

"I have seen to the *señora*'s things and her room is ready," Consuelo was saying. "Shall I show her upstairs now?"

"I'll take care of it," Wade told her. "I need to get cleaned up and change my clothes."

"I will serve dinner when you come down."

"Thanks, Consuelo." Wade took Joanna's arm and escorted her through the large kitchen, his warm grip distracting her from the efficiently arranged work areas and hanging utensils that might otherwise have claimed her attention. It wasn't until she made a deliberate effort to withdraw from Wade's touch that she felt in control of her senses once again.

Ignoring the faintly questioning look he threw her as she made a subtle move to free her arm, Joanna took in her surroundings with interest as Wade led her from the kitchen down a short hall to the spacious living room that dominated the ground floor.

Joanna hesitated a moment as she noted that the red tile that had begun in the kitchen continued on into this room. She would soon discover that it extended through the entire main floor. Heavy, brightly colored woven rugs were scattered here and there, and one larger rug was the centerpiece of the main furniture grouping in the middle of the room.

The whitewashed walls were hung with Western oils and watercolors, perfect accents to the masculine-looking leather furniture and chunky wooden tables that seemed almost as rough-hewn as the exposed wooden beams that striped the ceiling.

But it was the massive stone fireplace that commanded attention, the blackened Ten Star brand burned into the mantel a stamp of pride and possession. Wade gave her only a moment before he touched her arm again, signaling her to come along.

He didn't take her into any of the other downstairs rooms, of which there were several, including a formal dining room and a den. Instead he guided her quickly to the wrought-iron staircase that ascended from the red-tiled floor of the entry hall at the front of the house.

"The other indoor staircase leads down to the kitchen," he told her on their way up. "Megan and I generally use that one to save Consuelo extra work when we come in from the range." At the top of the stairs, he turned to the left. "Guest rooms are back the other way." He jerked his thumb in that direction. "This is Megan's room," he added as they passed a partially opened door that gave no more than a glimpse of a white ruffled bedspread. "And this one is yours."

Wade opened the door to a room that was much larger than she'd expected. Done in cheery pastel colors, mainly yellow, it was an instant lift to the spirits. Like all the floors upstairs, the floor was of lustrous dark-stained oak, an amber area rug softening the contrast between the gentle yellows and the dark wood of the floor and furniture. With pleasure, Joanna saw there was a floral-upholstered love seat and chair grouped together with a small low table in front of the double glass doors that opened onto the balcony.

"It's beautiful, Wade," she murmured as she ran a finger over the highly polished chest nearby, deeply appreciative of the fine quality of the furniture.

"There's something I'd like to say, Joanna." Wade's tone was serious and sent a shaft of apprehension through her that brought her head around. To her relief, he was no longer touching her, but he might as well have been, she realized as she tilted her chin up and her eyes met the odd intensity of his.

"You said something after we landed today," he went on, and Joanna knew instantly what he was talking about. She started to step away but Wade's hand shot out to stop her. "You said you thought I'd never brought you here because I was ashamed of you."

"Please don't say anything more," she murmured through stiff lips, unable to look at him. "I understand. Really."

"No, you don't." Now his voice had roughened. "And I'd appreciate it if you'd look at me when we talk." She was startled by his reproving tone and her eyes cautiously met his. "I don't like being frosted out."

Silence fell hard in the quiet room as momentary

shock gave way to a burst of resentment in Joanna. "And I think you're expecting a lot from me."

Wade's fingers were still wrapped around her arm, their firm pressure increasing fractionally at her words. "How so?"

The challenge she read in his gaze prodded at the barrier of her reserve, crumbling it a bit more. "I'm tired of being dragged around by a domineering, unfriendly stranger who would be happier if I didn't exist."

Joanna suddenly felt faint. She'd rarely spoken to anyone like that, and it was clear Wade hadn't expected her to, either, judging by the dull flush that edged his cheekbones. The tense emotional restraint between them snapped and flooded forth in a torrent of brutal honesty.

"I can't deny my life would be a hell of a lot simpler if you didn't exist," he agreed, releasing her. "But then again, without you, I wouldn't have the Ten Star."

"You'd still have it," she told him with conviction. "One way or another, you'd have found some way to keep it without marrying me."

Wade's mouth formed a bitter line. "That's right, I would have—if there'd been enough time. As it was, it wouldn't have been long before someone stepped in to claim everything. Marrying you and getting my hands on some working capital kept me solvent until I could start drilling for oil."

Wade was silent for a moment and Joanna's gaze fell from the penetrating intensity of his. "I'm not

proud of what I had to do to keep my ranch, Joanna.''
His statement didn't really surprise her. ''But I'd do
it again, given the same pressures and the same
choices.''

Joanna nodded her understanding, hearing the stubbornness in his voice. She felt a bit confused by her
admiration for his confession.

''I'm certain you would,'' she said, not quite able
to keep the resentment she felt from her tone.

''But I still owe you an explanation,'' he persisted.
''I never brought you over here, because frankly, I
was too wrapped up with both ranches to give you or
anyone else much thought until after the wedding.
Then, when your father died and you wanted to stay
on at the Double L till the funeral, I figured it could
wait a few more days. Looking back now, I admit I
must have seemed pretty callous.''

Joanna stood rigid, unable to suppress the memory
of her hurt and depression at the time. After the wedding ceremony, and her father's death just hours later,
Wade had taken her back to the Double L, at her
request. Though he'd spent the night, he'd slept
nearby in the guest room. The next morning, he'd
hired a housekeeper to stay at the ranch with her—a
babysitter, she'd thought bitterly. He'd spared a couple of hours to take her to make funeral arrangements,
but he hadn't insisted she move over to the Ten Star
before the funeral. In fact he'd seemed relieved at her
choice to spend those few days at the Double L.

''I just assumed you'd been over to the house at
one time or another. If I'd known you'd never been

here, I would have worked something out." Wade paused, then exhaled a deep breath. "I'm sorry."

Joanna felt her long-held anger begin to melt at those words. That Wade sincerely meant what he said was obvious to her, and she nodded her acceptance. Nothing positive would be accomplished between them if she hung on to her resentment.

"Consuelo doesn't like to keep supper too late, so I'd better go get cleaned up." Wade ran a restless hand through his dark hair. He had just turned to leave, when he stopped.

"You've guessed by now, haven't you, that our marriage won't be going on indefinitely?" How gently he spoke, yet how determined he seemed to get the subject into the open.

"Of course," she said, her voice as cool and undisturbed as she could make it. Inwardly, she felt the last of that old impossible fantasy shrivel and scatter like dust before the wind. Wade mumbled something to her then about the awkwardness of their situation, but Joanna couldn't quite hear over the unexpected twist of anguish in her heart.

"WHAT'S THE MATTER, sis? Did Jake put that burr under your saddle, or did I do something this time?" Wade's eyes were bright with teasing as he grinned down the table at his sister.

Megan had been in a temper from the moment she'd flounced into the dining room and plopped inelegantly onto her chair. Consuelo had just brought their steaks, but Megan sat petulantly over hers, jabbing and whacking at the meat. Joanna, who wouldn't have dreamed of putting on such a display, thought Megan was behaving like a spoiled brat.

"Jake Terrell has to be the most stubborn, mule-headed man in all of Texas," Megan burst out, and her steak knife made a mad slash through the air to punctuate her words.

Wade chuckled, as amused by his sister's temper as Joanna was apprehensive. She had always been uncomfortable around Megan, and it was distressing to be taking her first meal at the Ten Star while Megan was in such ill humor. Megan's lack of consideration didn't speak well of what living on the Ten Star would be like.

"What's he done this time?" Wade's question made it sound as if Jake managed to cross Megan regularly.

"He's not taking me to the dance Saturday night," she told her brother huffily.

"So? When have you ever gone without a date on a Saturday night?" Wade cut another chunk of the thick, juicy steak he'd been served, dismissing his sister's pique.

"Since I've been seeing Jake Terrell," Megan grumbled, chin in hand as she balanced the tip of her steak knife on the edge of her plate and rolled the handle between her fingers.

"He's a busy man, Megan. You know how much work it is to run a ranch."

"It's not *his* ranch," she reminded her brother as

she dropped her knife and crossed her arms over her chest.

"That's right. And that makes it harder for him to just drop everything and go paint the town every time you crook your finger." Wade's amusement with his sister's temper had waned. Now he spoke sternly and Joanna found it oddly reassuring.

"Running the Little Mesquite has nothing to do with taking me to the square dance Saturday night," Megan retorted with a disdainful toss of her head.

"How do you know?"

"Because." Suddenly Megan sounded a bit uncomfortable, and for the first time since she'd stormed into the room, she cast a glance in Joanna's direction. Joanna caught the look and politely returned her attention to her steak. Although her place had been set precisely halfway between Wade, who sat at the head of the long table, and Megan, who sat at the other end, she might as well have been invisible once Megan put in an appearance. Which, under the circumstances, was fine with Joanna.

"Does this have anything to do with that little tantrum you threw a couple of weeks ago?" Wade asked.

Megan's temper shot up again. "He knew I'd get over being angry and go to the dance with him," she fumed.

"And that's the point," Wade cut in. "Maybe he's tired of having to second-guess you every time you get your back up." He reached for his wineglass and took a sip. "I take it Jake's made other plans for Saturday night."

Megan's face flushed. "He's doing it just for spite," she grumbled.

"He's probably trying to teach you a lesson, Meg." Wade replaced his wineglass, his brow furrowed with disapproval. "And I think it's one you're overdue to learn."

Wade's face had gone grim, his eyes deadly serious. Joanna secretly admired the way he'd handled Megan's petulance, treating her first with indulgent affection, yet ultimately with gentle honesty.

Megan subsided, not completely—for she tossed her older brother a mutinous look now and then—but enough so the rest of the meal passed in relative peace.

They had almost finished eating when Consuelo stepped through the swinging doors from the kitchen. "*Señor*, Señora Kemp has just called. She would like to know if you could come over and look at one of her mares. She has been unable to reach either of the vets."

Wade was on his feet instantly. "Tell her I'll be right there." He downed the last of his wine in one swallow before he glanced Joanna's way. "I might not be back till late," he told her. "I'd like you to go out with me tomorrow, so it might be a good idea if you made it an early night. We generally eat breakfast at six." With that, Wade headed into the kitchen on his way out the back.

Joanna finished her steak, and reached for the glass of wine Wade had poured for her earlier. Tasting it, she put it down, feeling awkward and self-conscious now that she and Megan were alone together. Megan's green eyes were giving her the once-over, and Joanna sensed something was coming. In an effort to delay or elude whatever it was, she touched her napkin to her lips and laid it beside her plate, preparing to rise and retreat to her room for the night.

"How do you feel about my brother?"

Joanna went still at the question, then turned her head to meet Megan's curious gaze. All evidence of Megan's earlier tantrum was gone, but there was a shrewdness about her now that made Joanna almost wish she was still ranting about Jake.

Cautiously she answered, "I don't really know him very well."

"You don't have to know him well to fall in love with him," Megan countered.

Joanna got to her feet, signaling she was about to leave. "I don't think there's much chance of that happening."

Megan was leaning back in her chair now. "Well, just in case it does, perhaps there are one or two things you should know."

"I doubt that," Joanna said quickly, bravely returning the watchful look Megan was giving her.

"Señora Kemp—as Consuelo calls her—is known to most everyone else around here as Lorna," Megan informed her anyway. She added archly, "Four years ago, before our brother Chad died, and Wade found out how badly off the ranch was, she and Wade were pretty close." Megan watched Joanna's face with interest. "He was about to propose to her, but when he found out he'd have to marry you to save the Ten Star, he had to give her up. She married Ray Kemp just a few months after that.'' Megan affected a considering look, but the glimmer in her eyes was faintly cruel. ''Now that she's a widow, I think Wade's planning to ask her to marry him—after he works out his problems with you.''

Joanna marshaled every bit of cool she possessed and shrugged. ''That's really none of my business, is it?''

''It would be for me, if I was in your place,'' Megan told her. ''But then, I think my brother's had to wait long enough to be happy.''

Joanna took a small step to the side, then slid her chair closer to the table. ''If you don't mind, I think I will have an early night.''

''Why should I mind?'' came the smart reply.

Joanna turned then and went up to her room, her thoughts filled with unhappy speculation about the woman who would be the next Mrs. Wade Hollister.

CHAPTER THREE

JOANNA WALKED NEXT to Wade, her senses awash in fear. Every step took them nearer the barn and the disaster that was waiting; every stab of anxiety she felt was telling her so, promising it.

On this her first morning on the Ten Star she'd been late coming down for breakfast, and if that wasn't bad enough, Wade hadn't seemed in the best of moods. His foreman, Gene Frost, had joined them for the early meal. By the time she discovered that his plans for her that day included riding a horse, it was too late to tell him that the only time she'd ever been on a horse she'd fallen off, been hurt and never ridden again. Besides, Megan had been sitting at the table, and Joanna hadn't been able to muster the nerve to tell Wade, in front of Megan and the tough-looking foreman, that she didn't know how to ride and was panic-stricken at the thought.

So she was enduring her anxiety in silence, hurrying along beside Wade and Gene Frost, hoping for a lull in their conversation. It was during a moment of frustration, when Wade paused and the other man thought of something else, that Joanna happened to catch sight of Megan's face.

Mischief sparkled in the brunette's green eyes. Joanna only had to see the look to recognize why it was there. Either Megan knew she couldn't ride, or she had somehow guessed it. Whichever, Megan's silence told her that she was delighted by Joanna's dilemma, and relished the thought of Wade's irritation when he found out. That made Joanna even more certain that Wade's reaction would be explosive—something that Megan, with her impish sense of humor, would also enjoy.

"Wade, I'd like to tell you something," Joanna got out when they reached the barn and Frost went on.

Clearly still annoyed about something his foreman had just said, Wade's voice was brusque as he walked inside to the three horses that were standing saddled. "Can't it wait?"

Megan went in with him and got her horse, a glossy sorrel with a blaze face. Flaunting her horsemanship, she sprang onto the sorrel as if it were bareback, not bothering to use the stirrups until she was mounted. Joanna waited nervously just outside the wide doorway as Wade led a big gray and a sedate-looking bay toward her.

"This is Lucky," he said as he thrust the reins of the bay in her direction. Joanna reached for them hesitantly. "Let's get a move on." With that, Wade turned to mount the gray.

The size of the bay was intimidating, and as the big horse stretched his dark nose toward her and took a step forward, Joanna automatically took a step back, wary of his huge, iron-shod hooves. Curious, the big horse followed, stopping only when Joanna threw up a nervous hand to fend him off.

"I-is he gentle?" she stammered.

"One of the gentlest we own," Megan assured her, a barely suppressed grin on her lips.

"We've got a lot to get done this morning, Joanna." Wade's voice startled her edgy nerves. She glanced over to see he was already mounted. By the restless prancing of the gray, Joanna knew both were eager to be off, and the moment of choice—whether to tell Wade, or somehow bluff it out—had come.

"I'm not a good rider," she ventured, gripping Lucky's reins, trying to fight down her apprehension. All she could think of was the memory of climbing onto one of her father's horses, then falling off and being hurt.

"You'll improve," he told her, clearly impatient. "We're only riding a short time this morning since you need to get used to it gradually. Come on."

It wasn't as if she'd be spending the day on this horse, Joanna consoled herself. Wade was making some allowances for her, even if he didn't know the full extent of her inexperience. Surely she could handle that.

Only slightly relieved, she divided the reins and draped them over Lucky's neck. Noticing how high the top of the saddle was turned her knees to jelly, and if she'd been able, she might have given in to the crazy impulse to turn and run back to the house.

But she had to learn to ride. She'd never be able to learn about ranching if she remained safely at the house, much as she'd rather. Worse yet, she'd be a laughing stock in front of Megan and Wade and their macho Texas cowhands if she chickened out now. Perhaps she could just climb onto this horse and take it very easy for long enough to get over her fear and keep from falling off. Whispering a desperate prayer, she got a firm grip on the saddle and raised a booted foot to the stirrup.

It took more effort than she counted on, but she managed to lever her weight up enough to swing her right leg over Lucky's back and land awkwardly in the saddle. Getting her right foot in the other stirrup took a bit of doing, since she couldn't bring herself to actually lean to the side and see where her toe should go. At least the stirrups were the right length for her.

Lucky stood patiently beneath her, but to Joanna, every swish of his tail promised to unseat her. Her fingers were locked on the reins and saddle horn; her body was so stiff with fear that her muscles ached. She even gritted her teeth. She was unaware, however, of how pale her face was.

"Something wrong?" If Wade's voice had possessed even a small measure of tolerance for the way she was slowing him down, she might have been able to admit the truth. Daring to look up from the saddle horn that was her only anchor, she forced herself to relax. One glance at Megan's dancing eyes cemented her shaky decision to bluff it out. Besides, if Wade lost his temper and raised his voice now, Lucky might get spooked and run off with her just as her father's horse had done years ago.

"I'm fine." The weak, pasty smile on her mouth held Wade's attention for a few moments, but he wasted little time in starting the gray off at a walk, with Megan on her sorrel beside him. Lucky moved forward, too, then jerked to a stop so abruptly that Joanna was almost unseated.

As if she should have known better, Wade ordered curtly, "Let out on those reins."

Joanna struggled with fingers that refused to surrender their grip. Lucky tossed his head and started to turn around, confused by the erratic signals he was getting from Joanna. Panicked by the sudden movement, she hauled back harder on the reins and Lucky's front feet came off the ground.

In an instant, Wade pivoted his horse and reined in beside her. His strong arm hooked around her waist and plucked Joanna from Lucky's back just as she started to slip from the saddle. In the next wild heartbeat, she was sitting across Wade's lap clinging to him in sheer terror. No place on earth could have felt more secure, and Joanna clung tighter, snuggling a damp cheek against the warm, smooth flesh of Wade's neck.

"What's the matter with you?" he growled, as he lowered Joanna swiftly to the ground. His look was thunderous when he straightened.

It was as if her nearness repelled him, and she felt tides of humiliated color wash over her face. "I never learned to ride,'' she told him, choking back the sob that throbbed soundlessly in her chest.

Wade stared at her a moment, his dark expression unrelenting. Megan shifted in her saddle, calling attention to the amused grin on her face. Joanna's spine went rigid. She knew that by nightfall everyone on the Ten Star would hear about what had happened this morning.

"You what?" he demanded gruffly, his head tilted at an angle that suggested he might not have heard her correctly.

"I never learned to ride," she repeated, her slim shoulders straightening as she recovered her dignity.

"Why didn't you speak up?" he grumbled, then shook his head as the answer came to him. "Never mind." Wade looked over at his sister. "Take Lucky in to Hec." Then he said to Joanna, "You can go back to the house. We'll talk about this later." With that, he touched a spur to the gray and rode away.

Megan didn't stay around long, either, and leaned down to scoop up Lucky's reins and lead him into the barn. In a moment she was back out, tossing Joanna a laughing glance before she rode off at a lope to catch up with her brother.

Joanna stared after them, still shaken from the experience with Lucky, stunned by Wade's brusque behavior toward her. How could she have so docilely returned to Texas with him? Was this a taste of what living on the Ten Star would be like? The thought brought a flare of anger but, she reminded herself, she should have known what to expect. Wade cared nothing for her aside from the temporary obligation she represented. He had likely lost his temper with her just now because her inability to ride a horse would extend that obligation. And if there was one thing she'd understood from this traumatic little incident, it was that her very nearness repulsed him.

Joanna picked up her brown Stetson, then smoothed her hair away from her face. She almost put the hat back on, but changed her mind, feeling enough of a phony already in her cowboy boots and riding clothes when she hadn't managed to stay on Lucky for more than a few seconds. A quick glance around the ranch yard told her that there were only a couple of men about, working with some horses in a far corral. If they had seen her cowardice, they had tactfully gone on with their work.

Not wanting to go back to the house and risk Consuelo's questions about her quick return, Joanna stepped into the barn, grateful that Hec—whoever he was—was not around. Lucky was standing in the wide aisle that ran down the middle of the two-story structure, his head down, his eyes half-closed as if he were on the verge of taking a nap. His reins were looped over a peg and he hadn't been unsaddled.

Joanna moved closer, her light step rousing the animal and bringing his head up. Again the big horse stretched his nose in her direction, his ears perked forward, a friendly, benign look about him. Joanna forced herself to walk until she was within arm's reach of the animal. Lucky's red ears swiveled back, then forward again, as if he was expecting her to say something. Slowly, hesitantly, Joanna put out a hand and touched the white blaze that streaked down the gelding's face.

"Are you really one of the gentlest horses they own?" she asked softly. Lucky's liquid brown eyes seemed to confirm that. Joanna realized with chagrin that no matter how little Wade cared for her, he wouldn't have given her a horse that wasn't gentle.

And that made Joanna feel even worse. How would she ever live with these people if she couldn't get over her fear of riding? Wade and Megan had probably been riding since they were old enough to walk, and she could imagine how disgusting her lack of ability and her cowardice must be to them.

Her only chance of redeeming herself was to get over her fear and prove to them she had some backbone. An idea was forming in her mind, and though she tried to resist it, she couldn't resist its logic.

How many times had she heard the old saw about getting right back on a horse after you've been thrown? If she hadn't broken her wrist and got a concussion the time her father's horse had thrown her, she might have been encouraged to mount the animal again. She would have laid those old fears to rest long ago. Now, as an adult who was likely to live out her days on a ranch, she had to get over her fear and learn to ride well, or few of the people who would be working on the Double L would have any respect for her.

Grimly resigned, Joanna put on her hat, tugged it down to a determined angle, then reached over and untied Lucky's reins before she could talk herself out of it. Lucky nudged at her arm, then raised his head and blew softly in her face with his nostrils. Thinking this might be his way of making friends, she stood still, relaxing a bit as he gently inspected her.

When he finished, Joanna got a firm grip on the reins, then stepped slightly to the side and began to lead him. At first she gingerly avoided his hooves, but soon realized that he was in no danger of stepping on her. Before long she was able to face forward, delighted when he walked placidly at her side.

No one was near the deserted, steel-railed corral she had chosen, so Joanna led Lucky in and closed the gate. It was some time before she could work up the nerve to mount. Then, not giving herself a chance to change her mind, she gathered up the reins, got a good grip on the saddle and hoisted herself up.

To her surprise, sitting atop Lucky felt a bit more natural this time. Remembering what Wade had said about letting out on the reins, Joanna did so, not wanting to prompt Lucky to rear again. For several moments she sat very still, waiting for the tremors of fear to ease, waiting to summon the courage to urge Lucky into a walk. She remembered from her father's instructions years ago how to lay the reins along one side or the other of a horse's neck to get him to turn.

"Okay, Lucky," she murmured, tapping her heels ever so cautiously against the bay's sides. The big horse started forward at an easy walk around the corral, striding patiently around and around until the ground didn't look so far down to Joanna and her body slowly adapted to the rhythm of his movement.

When they reached the steel gate of the enclosure after several laps, Joanna pulled back gently on the reins.

Carefully she put out a hand and leaned down as far as she dared to reach the gate latch. Lucky stepped forward as the gate swung open, then walked through as if he were glad to be getting out of the corral. His eagerness brought a new wave of fear, but Joanna didn't panic. Lucky was headed in the direction Wade and Megan had ridden that morning, so Joanna didn't stop him, determined to face her fear once and for all. Surviving the next few minutes could mean freedom.

As her tension receded, Joanna became aware of the world beyond herself, Lucky and the grip she had on the saddle horn. At a couple of hours past dawn, the sky was deepening from a pale blue to cerulean; the morning air was cool, making her glad of her down vest and the thick flannel shirt beneath. Back at the house earlier, the temperature had been somewhere in the fifties, but the light breeze and her unaccustomed exposure to the spring air made her hunch her shoulders to hoard body warmth and warm her ears. She had always been one to chill easily and hadn't liked the often bitter winter cold of Iowa. She welcomed the thought of the predicted low-seventies temperature that had been forecast for later that day, judging that with the move to Texas she would at least experience more agreeable weather.

The corrals and outbuildings of the ranch became less numerous, until she had ridden Lucky well away from the earlier activity around the barns. Ahead were miles of endless, sometimes flat, sometimes rolling, prairie with an occasional spring-budded tree, and a sparse stand of what looked like cypress along a shallow streambed. Joanna's eyes were drawn by the slow arc of a hawk in the pale sky, and she watched for a moment as it swooped and circled, then dropped to a lone mesquite tree in the distance.

Lucky moved at a brisk walk for at least a mile and a half before Joanna relaxed enough to loosen her left hand on the saddle horn. When Lucky began to trot, then edged into a gentle canter, her grip tightened on the reins, but she allowed him to continue. It took concentration, but she managed to ride at that pace, instinctively tightening her legs around the horse's barrel while she kept a good hold on the saddle. When at last they rode over the long low crest of a shallow rise, she gasped and drew Lucky to a halt.

Three dozen horses bounded toward them from a quarter of a mile away. Driven by four wranglers, they were headed straight for the ranch, and she was directly in their path. Without conscious thought, Joanna tugged Lucky's reins to the side and dug in her heels, taking herself well out of the way to a place where she could watch.

As the horses thundered closer, their colors seemed to brighten from a blur of earth tones to grays, browns, and blacks. Four wranglers kept them in an organized bunch as they passed. Joanna recognized Wade and Megan among them.

Lucky pranced impatiently, and Joanna cautiously

allowed him to follow the small herd, keeping him at the slow canter she'd nearly mastered. She was able to follow closely enough to witness the last of the drive.

Just when it looked as if the leaders were on a straight path right to the open gate of one of the corrals, a pinto surged to the side and the horses directly behind him followed suit. Wade's gray leaped in to head him off, and the pinto shied back into position in time to be driven through the gate.

Joanna grinned with pleasure, exhilarated by the excitement as she rode nearer and watched the horses, which would be part of the roundup remuda, run around the inside of the enclosure, kicking up clods of damp earth as they circled and gradually slowed. When she reached the spot where Wade and Megan waited, her pleasure faded to uncertainty.

"What were you doing out there just now?" Wade demanded, his face once again dark and forbidding.

"I was—"

"You were out there in the way," he interrupted, his anger seeming to pulse in the air around him. "You could have been run down, or caused someone else to get hurt."

Joanna was stunned. "You were going to take me with you not two hours ago," she retorted.

"That was before I realized you couldn't ride," he growled. "And why couldn't you? You lived on the Double L for two years."

Joanna caught sight of the two wranglers Wade and Megan had been riding with and felt heat wash into her cheeks. Both of them had heard Wade's reproach and were ducking their heads, pretending they hadn't. One turned toward his horse and made a show of checking a cinch, the other simply led his animal out of earshot. Megan wasn't quite so gracious as she leaned back in her saddle, avidly interested in what Joanna would say.

"Does it matter now?" Joanna responded, not caring to satisfy Megan's interest, or Wade's, either, for that matter. Neither of them really wanted to know, and Joanna was not comfortable revealing the deep personal trauma that she and Lucky were slowly putting to rest. "I didn't learn to ride then, but I have now," she naively declared.

Megan tossed her head back and laughed. "There's a big difference between learning to ride well, and what you've been doing this morning, Joanna," she mocked. "And from the looks of it, we'll be lucky if you're a passably good rider by next winter."

Joanna met Megan's scorn with a composure that cloaked the destruction of her fragile confidence. She thought she'd done well this first time and had come to feel that since she'd nearly conquered her fear, practice would gain her a fair amount of competence with horses. It came as a shock to hear Megan's critical assessment of what she'd accomplished.

"That's enough, Megan," Wade said in a clipped aside to his sister. He turned to Joanna. "Go back to the barn and leave Lucky tied where you found him."

He was just about to ride away, when Joanna spoke. "I'd like to keep riding."

"Do as I say, Joanna." Wade looked at her severely. "You've tempted fate enough for one morning. I'll arrange some lessons for you when I get time and can spare someone." His eyes lingered briefly on her flushed features before the gray pivoted away and pranced smartly to the corral, effectively communicating his master's dismissal.

Self-consciously, Joanna turned Lucky and rode him down the dirt alley that led to the stable. She was deeply disappointed by Wade's reaction and as Megan's critical remarks came back to her, she wondered what she was doing wrong. Fortunately there was no one in the stable as she rode down the aisle and carefully dismounted. She was surprised at the painful protest of abused muscles as she slid to the ground, and then she walked stiffly to the house.

Later that morning, Joanna went to find Wade in the den. As she entered, she looked around, noting the bookshelves on one wall and an arched fireplace on the other. The room's only furniture was a leather couch in front of the bookshelves, one wing chair and footstool before the fireplace and a massive desk in front of the window.

Wade was standing in front of the hearth, staring up at the detailed, hand-drawn map of the Ten Star that hung over the mantel. Joanna didn't speak at first, just watched him, knowing full well that although he seemed to be ignoring her, he couldn't possibly be so obtuse.

He was still angry with her; she'd sensed that instantly. There was a suppressed energy about him that made her wary of nettling him further. But she was also aware that what she'd seen of his volatile temper was triggering a like tendency in her.

The facade of reserve she had come to think was impervious was crumbling and, she thought bitterly, Wade Hollister was the person responsible. Why now, after all these years, did her emotions—particularly anger—boil so close to the surface? Why did the thought of a confrontation with Wade invigorate her instead of frighten her? Joanna's introspective thoughts ended the moment Wade turned to face her, his blue eyes arrowing straight into hers.

"I'd like to talk to you," she said, holding his gaze with a glittering intensity that matched his own.

"What about?"

"About this morning." She slipped icy fingers into her jeans pockets. "I don't like being scolded in public."

"You weren't scolded in public," Wade argued, his look chiding.

"Two of your men were there, and so was Megan," Joanna reminded him.

"Is that all?"

Wade was clearly dismissing her complaint and her. His arrogance was the prod that goaded her to continue. "No, that's not all," she said, then took a steadying breath. "I think we should be divorced as soon as possible."

Wade didn't respond immediately, but ran irritable fingers through his hair as he gave her a long, considering look. He was thinking seriously about her statement, she could tell. His next words surprised her.

"Not right away. Not until I'm comfortable turning the Double L over to you to run with a foreman."

"I'm releasing you from that agreement," she said quickly. "As long as the Double L is operating at a profit and all its assets are restored, the bargain you made with my father is fulfilled to my satisfaction."

"I gave Will my word," Wade informed her, his face turning hard. "I won't file divorce papers until the bargain has been fulfilled to *my* satisfaction."

"I don't want to wait that long."

"It won't be long," he assured her grimly. "Not a day longer than I think is necessary."

Joanna bristled. "Then it won't be up to you," she said. "I'll file the papers myself."

"Like hell you will," he blustered, and took a step toward her. "I owe your father too much."

"That may be," she agreed. "But I don't believe it's possible for you to teach me anything."

"Why not?" he demanded roughly.

Joanna took an uneven breath. She wanted to tell him it was because he was too harsh with her, too domineering, that she didn't like being bullied and treated like an unpleasant obligation. Thanks to her father, she'd had enough of that treatment for one lifetime. But there was something more deeply painful about Wade's actions that she wanted to confront him about—something that struck at her as a woman. It was perhaps the main reason he behaved as he did toward her.

"You can barely stand to have me around you, Wade," she said boldly, frightened, yet feeling a tiny release of the anger and bitterness she'd kept to herself since childhood. "I think my presence irritates you."

The room went still, and Joanna's heart pounded in her chest. She knew Wade was furious. The anger emanating from him gave him a dangerous aura that made her want to step back. Only by sheer force of will did she manage to stand her ground. Wade was only angry because she had guessed the truth and had dared to tell him so.

Wade stared at the small, riled female before him, who'd managed to throw his future into chaos, pitching him into an emotional uncertainty he'd never dreamed he'd experience. From the moment he saw her just four days before, she had managed to wedge herself into a part of his heart reserved only for Lorna. And it was time to put a stop to all that, time to clarify for them both that what he was feeling was little more than the basest of emotions.

"I think you've defined the real problem, Joanna," he said at last, his voice a low drawl as he stepped forward and wrapped powerful, lean fingers around her upper arms. Joanna tried to pull back but couldn't, throwing her hands up against his chest in self-defense.

"I can't seem to stand having you around me," he readily admitted, and Joanna felt a stab of pain. "And when I think how difficult the next few weeks or months are going to be, it does tend to make me a little irritable.''

Joanna pushed hard against his chest, wanting to escape him, unbearably hurt, suffering an agony she hadn't felt this deeply in years. It took everything she had to hold back the tears that seared behind her eyes, while she tried to numb herself to the heated sensations that pulsed through her body just because Wade was touching her. She must be demented, she thought, to feel so sexually attracted to him now.

''Maybe I should do something to soothe that irritation. What do you think, Joanna?'' he breathed as he pulled her fully against his long, hard body. ''And you are an irritation to have around...but not in the way you think.''

Joanna had little more than a moment to consider his words. In the next, conscious thought spiraled away from her as his head descended and he laid his lips against hers, tenderly caressing their softness with the firm expertise of his.

''Let me in, Joanna,'' he urged in a rough whisper. ''Open your mouth.'' Shocked senses plunged into a molten stream like hot lava as the initial touch of his tongue against hers stole her strength and shattered her reserve. She was gloriously alive one instant, then dying a sweetly torturous death the next as his tongue teased, then coaxed, then demanded to mate with hers.

Frantic fingers slipped up his taut cotton shirtfront to spear wildly into his black hair. Instinctively Joanna used her hands to lever her mouth more fully

onto his, unconscious of the greedy passion she was
betraying.

Suddenly she was thrust away from him, away
from the source of the sensual awakening that still
flooded through her in wave upon wave of raw
delight. Never had she felt so deprived, and never had
she felt quite so thoroughly rejected. A new kind of
pain slashed through her as she opened dazed hazel
eyes to the furious gunmetal hardness of Wade's.

"Lust can cause a lot of problems for us, Joanna.
It can start things that have no business getting
started, and it can sure as hell make problems for us
that neither of us need." Wade released her, and she
staggered back a step, pale with humiliation as she
took a quick, deep breath and struggled to recover her
senses.

Her expression seemed to soften him. "I'm sorry,
Joanna. That was uncalled for," he allowed gruffly.
"And I had no right to treat you harshly earlier." He
released a frustrated breath. "This whole damned situation is awkward enough, and I just made it worse."

He reached out a hand in a gesture of apology, but
Joanna knocked it away.

"Oh, there you are, big brother," Megan called
from the doorway as she sailed into the den and
tossed herself onto the leather couch. "I didn't interrupt anything…important, did I?"

Joanna could hear the false innocence in Megan's
voice and realized she must have either seen or overheard what had just taken place. Not surprisingly that
made Joanna feel even more shamed by her response

to Wade and the brutal way he'd rejected her. She needed to get away from them both.

She turned, spine rigid, chin lifted with feigned dignity, and started to leave the room.

"Consuelo serves lunch in five minutes, Joanna," Megan called after her, but Joanna doubted she'd have much of an appetite.

CHAPTER FOUR

THE NEXT THREE WEEKS passed in silent torment as Joanna struggled with the tempestuous, yet fruitless feelings Wade's kiss had aroused. It was, she realized grimly, a lot like restoring circulation to a numbed limb and enduring the pins-and-needles agony of re-awakening.

She'd never been kissed before—at least not the way Wade had kissed her. Her only prior experience had been at a company Christmas party in Des Moines when one of the salesmen had got a little too drunk and had given her a sloppy, weak-lipped kiss beneath the mistletoe—a kiss not worthy to be compared with the mating of lips Wade had given her. To be so carelessly initiated into a realm of sensuality she hadn't thought possible for her seemed cruel, since she wasn't likely ever to experience more of it than in those all too brief moments in Wade's arms.

Consequently each moment she spent with Wade seemed more awkward than ever. He was just as laconic as he'd always been, though much less stern. But a look passed between them now and again, a look of recollection and, though Joanna would not have defined it as such, of primal recognition.

Mostly, however, except for her riding lessons with him, Wade left her to her own devices. Following the lessons, nearly all her time was spent on horseback, something that both she and Wade had determined was the quickest way for her to improve.

After nearly three weeks of lessons and countless forays into the range that surrounded the ranch head-quarters, Joanna rode for hours at a stretch, her body adjusted to the exercise, her confidence growing in proportion to her skill. Each night she collapsed wearily onto her bed by seven, only to find sleep eluded her for hours, her body seized with a longing she could only lie awake and endure.

Wade frequently went out for the evening—to see Lorna, Megan made certain Joanna knew—and Joanna often didn't sleep soundly until she heard Wade's footsteps in the hall as he passed her room on the way to his.

Today had been another long tiring day, and as a light April rain pelted her yellow rain slicker, Joanna trudged toward the ranch house that had strangely rooted itself in her mind as home.

Home. Joanna smiled bitterly to herself. If the Ten Star was home, then it was a cold, friendless one. She was an outsider here, just as she'd been at her aunt's house, just as she'd been at the Double L with her father. Whenever she walked into Consuelo's kitchen after an afternoon's absence, the woman would glance her way and smile. Then, with a politeness that held Joanna at a distance, Consuelo would murmur some word of greeting and continue on with her work.

This evening, Joanna hesitated as she reached for the doorknob, not eager to face the indifference inside. Forcing her mouth into a smile to match the perfunctory one she would receive from Consuelo, Joanna took the doorknob and gave it a twist.

"Howdy there." Jake Terrell was leaning against the kitchen counter, his eyes lighting up as Joanna came through the door.

"Hello, Jake," she said, pleased he was here, her spirits lifting at the warmth in his brown eyes. Feeling her weariness evaporate, she peeled off her slicker and the light jacket beneath, then hung them on a peg below the one that held her hat. "Good evening, Consuelo," she added softly.

"Good evening, *señora*," Consuelo responded, then waved a metal spatula toward the large hand that lifted a finger of chocolate icing from the cake she was frosting. "Out of that, Señor Jake," she scolded good-naturedly, "or there will be nothing left for the others."

"Yeah, maybe I'd better leave a little," Jake responded with a chuckle as he tasted the icing. "Lorna loves this stuff as much as I do."

A thread of apprehension coursed through Joanna at Jake's words, spoiling her enjoyment of seeing the affectionate byplay between Jake and the normally subdued Consuelo.

"Have you met Lorna Kemp yet?" he asked her, and Joanna shook her head, trying to ignore the close look he was giving her. She happened to catch the swift, nervous glance Consuelo shot her way.

"I think I'd better get cleaned up," she told them both, then stepped past Jake on her way to the staircase at the side of the kitchen.

After a hot, reviving shower, Joanna took special care with her makeup. Her hair at last the way she wanted it, its bouncing curls rioting around her head, she went to her closet to choose a dress.

Although no one had said so specifically, she assumed from Jake's remark that Lorna was to join them for dinner, or at least for a visit this evening. Not surprisingly she wanted to look her best. She finally selected a simple, long-sleeved buff-brown dress. It was nipped in at the waist beneath a silver concha belt, then flared into soft gathers that fell to just below her knees, brushing the top of the brown dress boots she'd bought in San Antonio. A turquoise bracelet, which fastened easily over the deep cuffs at her wrists, completed the casual Western look. After giving her hair and makeup one last look, Joanna hurriedly headed downstairs.

Wade and Jake stood at the bar near one corner of the living room, mixing drinks for Megan and a small, reed-thin blonde who sat next to Megan on the wide sofa. Joanna entered the room cautiously, more aware of her role as intruder than at any time since she'd returned to Texas.

"And here's Joanna." It was Jake who saw her first and spoke. Wade glanced in her direction, then froze a moment with his drink raised to his lips before he downed it in a single swallow. Megan looked up, and judging by the way her pert mouth slanted, she was relishing the whole situation.

Lorna turned her head and smiled when Joanna halted uncertainly at the edge of the furniture grouping. There was a long awkward silence as Wade continued to stare at her, his darkening gaze going over her from head to foot. Joanna suspected that her presence was embarrassing him, and wished at that moment she'd remained in her room.

"Lorna," Jake began, easing tactfully into the dreadful silence, "I don't think you've ever met Wade's wife, Joanna." The quick smile that came to Lorna's soft mouth was genuine, catching Joanna off guard as Jake made the introductions.

"It's nice to meet you," Joanna murmured quietly.

"And nice to meet you, Joanna. I apologize for calling Wade away from you so often the past few weeks," Lorna surprised her by saying. "I hated to intrude on the two of you now that you're back together, but everything that could possibly go wrong at my ranch is doing it this spring, I'm afraid. Thanks to your husband, I think things will run much more smoothly now, and I won't be such a bother to both of you."

"It was good that Wade could help. I don't mind," Joanna murmured with a smile. Her thoughts raced back to what Lorna had just said. *Now that you're back together?* Joanna glanced curiously at Wade.

"You're no bother," Wade assured Lorna in a low voice from where he leaned casually against the bar.

Joanna caught the discomfort that crossed his face as he flashed her a look.

"Yes, I am, Wade," Lorna protested, turning soft, doelike brown eyes toward him. "But you're too good a friend to complain."

"What can I get you to drink, Joanna?" Wade asked her then. Surprised that he was acknowledging her presence even that much, after rudely having allowed someone else to introduce her to his guest, Joanna shook her head and murmured a quiet thank-you. She slipped onto a nearby chair, prepared to be relegated to the background for the remainder of the evening.

So much for the extra pains she'd taken with her appearance, she thought, glancing enviously at the slim blonde who had swiftly reclaimed Wade's attention.

Lorna was dressed in a simple pink shirtdress belted with a narrow sash at the waist, and the effect was an effortless elegance and unpretentious style that Joanna believed she could never achieve. Yet there was a down-home look about Lorna, too, a homespun warmth and generosity of spirit that had no doubt made her many friends. Joanna couldn't dislike a woman like Lorna. Even knowing Wade was in love with Lorna and intended to marry her after he divorced Joanna had little effect on her initial impression of the woman, or the way she had instantly liked her.

"How're those riding lessons coming?" Jake asked as he strode over and eased his length onto a chair next to hers. Joanna hesitated a moment, hoping Wade had heard the question and would give some indication of what he thought.

"Slow," Megan cut in, having got to her feet in order to saunter over and seat herself on the arm of Jake's chair. The possessive hand she laid on his shoulder signaled she was claiming Jake for her own. "I doubt she'll be good enough to go on roundup."

Megan's words didn't really surprise Joanna, since Megan never passed up an opportunity to belittle her accomplishments. Nevertheless, Joanna couldn't help thinking, would it have hurt Megan to say something a bit kinder in front of guests?

Joanna merely shrugged vaguely, not willing to challenge Megan's assessment and make herself a target for the brunette's sarcasm. Looking away momentarily to see Wade join Lorna on the sofa, Joanna missed the way Jake leaned forward and rested his elbows on his knees, effectively removing Megan's hand from his shoulder.

"Wade told me the other day how well you're doing," Jake persisted, drawing Joanna's attention. "He says you're learning fast."

Jake's words surprised her, and she glanced quickly at Wade for confirmation. But he hadn't heard, absorbed as he was in what Lorna was saying to him now that they were sitting only a few inches apart. Joanna forced herself to meet Jake's gaze.

"He never says anything about it to me," she answered, uncertain how to respond to what he'd just said. She never knew what Wade really thought, but it pleased her to discover he'd said something positive to Jake about her.

"Señor Hollister," Consuelo called softly from the doorway, and Wade looked up. "Dinner is ready whenever you are."

"Thank you, Consuelo." Wade got to his feet, as did everyone else, but before he could take Lorna's arm, she'd started toward the dining room unescorted. Jake was swiftly claimed by Megan, and Joanna followed slightly behind them.

"Joanna?" Wade's voice was a quiet rasp, and Joanna turned her head to see what he wanted. Her eyes fell to the arm he offered, then shot back up to catch the look he was giving her.

Mutiny flared within her at the suspicion that Wade's gesture was a grim duty for him, one that he needed to discharge because he had a guest who might think less of him if he didn't. She ignored his arm and walked in alone, as Lorna had, silently taking her customary place at the table.

Thanks to Jake, who sat between her and Megan, but mostly to Lorna, Joanna enjoyed the meal, marveling how good food tasted when you shared it with people who didn't resent your presence. She found herself talking easily to Lorna, as the woman related her first experiences as a small-town accountant's daughter suddenly turned ranch wife—a situation not unlike Joanna's, Lorna was quick to point out. It was later, after Lorna began talking directly about her late husband, Ray, who'd died only the year before, that

Joanna saw the first glimmers of deep grief in her eyes.

"Gosh, I'm sorry," Lorna said to Joanna, then again to the others around the table. She attempted a shaky smile. "I'm afraid I still get a little carried away when I start talking about Ray. I wish you could have met him, Joanna."

"I'm sorry I didn't," Joanna told her sincerely, wanting to say something to ease the pain in her new friend, at a loss to know what. "He must have been a very special man."

"One of the best," Lorna assured her, her voice wobbling before she seemed to get a hold on her emotions.

Then Lorna began talking brightly again, her moment of grief seemingly passed, but all the more poignant for Joanna because she sensed that no matter how lighthearted the facade Lorna presented, the young widow was still in mourning for her husband.

Joanna didn't miss the gentle sympathy that came into Wade's eyes, or the blatant longing that shadowed their depths before he managed to shield it. Joanna realized then that he and Lorna were not having an affair—not when Lorna was still grieving. Perhaps Wade loved Lorna enough to keep his true feelings for her hidden, and was patient enough to play the part of a good friend and neighbor until she recovered from her husband's death. Could he be hoping, Joanna asked herself, that when that time came, Lorna would naturally fall in love with him again?

Megan had told Joanna that Wade and Lorna had

been close once and that he'd planned to propose to her before Chad died and he found out he was about to lose the Ten Star. According to Megan, Wade had given up Lorna to marry Joanna, then had had to stand by silently later when Lorna fell in love with Ray Kemp and married him.

Joanna glanced often in Wade's direction during the meal. She felt oddly relieved that no matter how little their marriage vows meant to him, he and Lorna obviously hadn't become lovers since Ray Kemp's death. Of course, that was probably more because of Lorna's grief than Wade's restraint. Still, the fact that he'd secretly suffered his love for Lorna for years and done nothing to threaten either her marriage or his own as long as Ray Kemp was alive and he was still trapped in his own bad marriage, was to his credit. Doubtless there were men who wouldn't have thought twice about seducing a married woman, or who would have taken advantage of a young, vulnerable widow and her dependence on their assistance, but Wade was apparently not one of them. Joanna finished her chocolate cake in thoughtful silence.

"Next time Wade comes over, come along with him," Lorna said to Joanna an hour or so after they'd moved back into the living room for coffee.

"I'd like that very much," Joanna responded noncommittally. She doubted she and Wade would be going anywhere as a couple—especially not to Lorna's. Joanna hadn't been away from the ranch since she'd arrived, not even to visit the Double L.

"Of course, you don't have to wait until Wade

comes by," Lorna went on. "Just ask him to give you directions, and drive on over yourself."

"Well, thank you," Joanna murmured, pleased by the invitation. She couldn't tell Lorna now that she'd never learned to drive, because instinctively she wanted to hide that fact from Wade. If she were lucky, Megan wouldn't recall that she hadn't taken driver's ed when they were in high school together.

"I hope you and Wade don't mind if I head home early," Lorna said apologetically after a while, again linking Joanna's name with Wade's as if Joanna was her hostess instead of Megan. "I didn't get much sleep last night, and I'm afraid today is beginning to tell on me."

"I understand," Joanna told her, her smile rueful. "I'm getting accustomed to early nights myself."

"Wait until roundup," Lorna grumbled good-naturedly as she and Joanna got to their feet. Everyone else rose then, and Megan went to get Lorna's jacket.

"Please bring mine, too, Megan," Jake called after her, then turned to Lorna. "Can I give you a ride home?"

"That would be nice, Jake," Lorna answered. "It would save Wade another trip tonight."

"It's no trouble, Lorna," Wade cut in quickly, the tenderness in his eyes as he looked down at her almost worshipful. To Joanna's amazement, Lorna seemed genuinely unaware of it.

"No, Wade," Lorna refused firmly. "You need to spend more time with your wife. Now that I've finally gotten to meet Joanna, I can't imagine how I could have caused you to leave her home alone so often.'' Then to Joanna, ''Thank you, Joanna, for having me to supper. And be sure to tell Consuelo again for me that no one makes better chocolate cake than she does.''

''We're so glad you could come,'' Joanna replied uneasily. She was uncomfortably aware that not only had someone else arranged for Lorna to be a dinner guest, they had overlooked mentioning it to her. It seemed to her dishonest somehow to masquerade as hostess when everyone but Lorna knew otherwise. And yet Joanna could think of no tactful way to clear up Lorna's misconception. ''You, too, Jake,'' Joanna added as she turned her head to look up into Jake's handsome face.

To her surprise, just as Megan returned, Jake bent down and kissed Joanna lightly on the mouth. ''G'night, Joanna,'' he said. ''I'll be seein' you.''

Joanna blushed at the gesture. Subdued, as the last of the farewells were made, Joanna couldn't meet anyone's gaze for long and was greatly relieved when Jake and Lorna were finally out the door.

A charged silence filled the small entry hall as the door closed. Joanna turned and came face-to-face with Megan's hostile look; she could almost feel animosity shooting toward her like sparks. Megan abruptly turned on her heel and headed straight for the staircase, thumping out her displeasure on the carpeted stairs before it dawned on Joanna what was wrong.

Jake had kissed her good-night and not Megan.

Joanna automatically looked to Wade, but his granite countenance seemed to underscore Megan's ire. She mumbled something awkward about being tired and brushed past him to hurry upstairs.

Whatever her hope had been of diplomatically smoothing Megan's ruffled feathers, it was dashed when her soft knock on Megan's door went unanswered.

The sound of Wade's booted feet coming up the stairs didn't register until he'd nearly reached the top. By then, Joanna had walked to her room and was just slipping inside. Wade's big hand caught the door and kept it from closing. "Invite me in."

Her first impulse was to refuse. Wade's and Megan's lack of courtesy toward her that evening had hurt deeply. Then again, Wade looked as if a refusal would make no difference at all to him. Joanna stepped aside and let him push the door open and enter the room.

"I'm tired," she reminded him as she started to edge away. "It's been a long day." But steel fingers wrapped around her arm as she took her next step, and Joanna drew back in alarm.

"What is there between you and Terrell?" Wade demanded roughly.

"Nothing," she heard herself say, too wary of Wade's temper to think of refusing to answer. "He's just a friend."

"Friends don't act like you two do," Wade accused.

Joanna felt a quick surge of anger. "What's sauce for the gander is sauce for the goose," she replied. "Isn't that what people would say in a case like this?"

"What do you mean by that?" he asked gruffly.

Joanna began to tremble and forced herself to go on. "There aren't many men who could tactfully entertain the woman they're in love with while their wife is present."

"That wasn't my idea," Wade grumbled. "It was Megan's doing."

Joanna nodded then, a bitter twist to her lips. "That I can believe."

"Which brings us back to you and Jake," Wade persisted.

Joanna bristled, her arm tensing against Wade's hold. "I haven't said a word to you about your, er, friendship with Lorna or any other woman. I expect the same courtesy from you regarding any male friends I might make."

Wade's grip tightened. "You're still my wife, Joanna," he reminded her grimly.

"I'm your wife when it's convenient for you, you mean," she tossed out, then quailed inside as Wade's expression turned severe.

"That's right," he admitted arrogantly. "And as long as it's convenient for me to be married to you, I won't have you becoming involved with another man."

"I doubt that's even possible," she said, not quite able to believe she was attractive enough to any man for that to happen. Her father's rejection had undermined her confidence where men were concerned.

"The hell it's not," he bit out. "The smell of money is a pretty strong draw."

Joanna was confused for a moment. She wasn't used to giving her inheritance much thought since she'd been forced to place most of it into the hands of a virtual stranger. "I guess you're right," she conceded slowly, knowing he was, but resenting his telling her to her face that money was the only thing about her a man could find attractive. "It drew you."

"Yes, it drew me," he said as he tugged her against him. "But you're getting every penny of it back and a fortune besides. The next man might not be so generous."

"So? What business will it be of yours?" she challenged incautiously.

Wade was silent for a moment, but Joanna sensed he was about to explode. She was released with a suddenness that caught her off balance for a second. "None," he snarled. "None at all."

"That's good," she shot back, riled, a little frightened, yet feeling more alive and more confident than she had in her entire life. "Because I don't think I like you much, Wade Hollister. I don't want you involved in any part of my life, much less my private life, and I'm counting the minutes until I no longer have to put up with either you or your ill-mannered sister."

Both stood in rigid silence, stiff with anger. Their

gazes remained locked in a duel of wills neither of them had expected.

"That's fine with me, Joanna," he growled at last, his eyes taking on a chilling gleam. "But until our business is concluded, you'd be wise to avoid getting involved with another man—particularly Jake Terrell."

"And what's wrong with Jake?"

"Not a thing. Except that you happen to be married to me."

Some of the rigidity left her at that, and a knowing smile twisted her lips. "I think I understand. You don't want to be embarrassed should it get around that the wife you don't want prefers someone else to you." Joanna laughed bitterly. "What a frail ego you have, Wade. I doubt if anyone, outside of a few of your men and your guests tonight, even knows you have a wife."

"Everyone in this part of Texas knows about you."

Wade's words took her aback momentarily, his abrasive tone sending a shiver of dread through her. "What could they possibly know about me?" Quiet now, subdued, she gave voice to the uppermost question in her mind.

Wade callously shattered her frail hope that she wasn't quite as notorious as his words implied. "They know you were an immature child when I married you, and that you ran off after your father died because marriage didn't suit you." Wade paused only a second at her quick indrawn breath. "They know you're back, and everyone assumes you've come to your senses and returned home to be with your husband.''

Joanna was silent for a long time. ''I take it no one has any idea that ours wasn't a match made in heaven,'' she concluded with a sarcasm normally alien to her.

''No one knows for certain why I married you,'' he said darkly.

Joanna forced her lips into a thin smile. ''Of course not. The truth wouldn't be too flattering to the Hollister name.'' Joanna made to brush past him when his hand shot out and roughly forced her to stay.

''I want your word that the truth won't come out.''

Again a bitter smile etched Joanna's lips. ''Don't worry. Your reputation is safe with me.''

Wade's grip tightened, anger bringing a dull flush to his face. ''It's not *my* reputation, it's Chad's. Your word, Joanna,'' he prompted with a slight shake of her arm, which brought her chin up defiantly.

''I would never tell anyone about something like that,'' she said, hurt that Wade thought she would reveal to anyone that his dead brother's gambling obsession had nearly broken the Hollisters, and forced Wade to marry a child for her money.

''Good.'' The steel fingers relaxed.

''And I'd appreciate some of the same consideration from you,'' she added swiftly.

Wade's eyes went hard. ''What kind of consideration?''

Joanna tugged her arm from his grip. ''I'd like you

to remember that I'll be living on the Double L, perhaps for the rest of my life.''

"What's that got to do with anything?'' he asked, clearly impatient with her.

"If everybody in this part of Texas believes what you said they do about me, how do you expect me to be able to make any kind of life for myself here? You want me to help protect your brother's reputation, but I think it's only fair that you and your sister show some consideration for mine.''

Joanna didn't wait for a response from Wade, but instead stepped away and turned toward the dresser, her frosty manner dismissing him.

"Aren't you going to leave?'' she asked, then glanced at his stern reflection in the dresser mirror as she unclasped her silver-and-turquoise bracelet and laid it gently in her jewelry box. "I've told you twice now that I'm tired.''

"We weren't finished.''

"I was.''

Wade's expression didn't alter at her defiance. It didn't need to; it was harsh enough. Joanna reached for the clasp on her concha belt, thinking he would take the hint and leave. To her sudden unease, his eyes followed the movement, then softened, staring openly at her fingers on the belt, then rising to the soft, full outline of her breasts.

Joanna, too, was unable to look away from the reflection, and her fingers stilled as her gaze began to stray over the virile image that shadowed hers.

Wade was such a big man, strong and hard, as if

cut from stone by the elements. His face and hands were already tanned from months in the west-Texas winter sun, his body so lean and fit that it was roped with rawhide-tough muscles. Next to him, Joanna felt small and delicate, the feminine complement to the powerful masculinity that seemed to radiate from him.

And he was looking at her, staring in such an erotically intense way that she felt both breathless and on fire with the sudden intuition that she wasn't the only one affected by a mirror image.

Wade turned abruptly and took one long stride toward the door, jamming his hands irritably into his pockets.

"You and I are invited to a barbecue a week from Saturday. But judging from your conduct tonight..." Wade let his words trail off meaningfully.

"There was nothing wrong with my conduct," she said with quiet dignity, "unless you're faulting me for coming down for dinner at all. But perhaps that's the point." Joanna briskly removed her belt and laid it in a tinkling heap on her dresser. She figured Wade was trying to find a semipolite way to ask her not to embarrass him by insisting on going to the barbecue. Criticizing her alleged bad conduct tonight was the obvious lead-in to that particular request, and Joanna found herself unwilling to let him think he was getting away with anything. Unmasking his motives was a small bit of retaliation for her. "Just remember when you make an excuse for my absence that I might get to meet those people someday."

She guessed she had hit her mark when she heard

Wade's colorfully descriptive curse. Then he was slamming out of her room. Joanna sagged gratefully against the dresser, trembling with relief that she had survived the confrontation, shocked beyond words at the new, but persistent, streak of audacity she'd somehow discovered within herself.

CHAPTER FIVE

JOANNA FIDGETED with the belt loop of her jeans as she forced her gaze to move from one weathered face to another of the dozen or so Double L ranch hands who stood before her.

Except for the cook, most were dressed in cotton shirts, jeans, boots and chaps. Several had come in from the range earlier than usual, because of the severe storm building to the west. A few carried yellow rain slickers; all wore Stetsons in various stages of age and use, which, she noted, they had removed in a show of respect as Wade briskly introduced her.

Joanna felt tongue-tied and embarrassed, automatically comparing the hands' seasoned cowboy clothing and manner against the too new, store-bought, tenderfoot image she knew she projected.

She decided to follow her natural instincts to acknowledge that image. "I recognize a few faces," she began, raising her voice as thunder rumbled ominously in the distance and the wind began to pick up, "but I'm not the best when it comes to remembering names. Please don't hesitate to correct me if I make a mistake." She faltered, clenching one small hand as she took a shaky breath and made her eyes meet the stares directed at her. "I don't know a lot about ranching," she admitted, "so I've got a lot to learn."

At that point, Joanna caught sight of Wade's stern profile, and her tongue seemed to stick to the roof of her mouth. He wasn't happy with her, but that wasn't exactly new. Though he'd apologized that morning for his behavior the night before, her cool response to his effort had driven a larger wedge between them. Now it was next to impossible to ignore both Wade and the threatening sky, which was beginning to lower and roll while she continued her brief, nervous speech.

"I'd really appreciate your patience until I get oriented," she went on. "I'll be relying a lot on your foreman, Bill Black, but I hope you won't mind answering any questions I might have about your work, or how things are usually done on the Double L." Joanna released her hold on the unfortunate belt loop and shoved her fingers into her jeans pockets in an agony of distress, unable to think of anything even remotely clever or bright to say that would change those expressionless faces into friendly ones. "Thank you."

It was a moment before anyone moved. Then, after several of the men looked in Wade's direction as if to seek his consent, they stepped forward and filed past as Wade introduced them. Joanna received a handshake and a polite nod or word of good luck from each man, while she tugged her hat lower to counter the gusty, rain-scented wind that tried to pull it off. The first big drops began to pelt down on them just as the last ranch hand in line spoke to her. The gathering broke up as the men donned their slickers and rushed off to secure the barns and livestock against the approaching storm.

Seconds later the skies suddenly opened up, and Wade seized Joanna's arm and hurried her toward the pickup, opening the door and shoving her in and along the seat ahead of him.

"Might as well get that slicker on," he said as he tossed her one of the yellow bundles from the floor and grabbed the other for himself.

Joanna wrestled on the stiff garment and peered through the spattered and streaked windows into the wind-whipped deluge outside. "We aren't going back to the Ten Star now?" she asked.

"What's that?" Wade crammed his hat back on and leaned toward her. The drumming of the rain on the metal roof of the truck was intensifying.

"Aren't we going to start for the Ten Star?" she repeated, raising her voice to ensure he could hear her over the din.

"Not now," he answered grimly as he turned away and cranked the window of the truck down an inch or so.

Joanna sat higher on her side of the seat, trying to look past his dark head to the open window. The rain was falling so hard that it was impossible to see much, not even the big barn. In fact the only thing visible to them was the section of board fence five feet from Wade's side of the truck.

Then, surprisingly, the rain began to let up.

"Don't get too comfortable," Wade muttered just as she started to lean back against the seat. "Let's go." He levered the passenger door open and stepped out. Joanna automatically scooted out after him, landing feetfirst in the puddle just below the running board of the truck. Grateful for her high-topped boots, she slogged through that puddle, then splashed through several more, trying not to slip and fall in the slick mud that was everywhere. By the time they reached the barn, they were both mud-spattered to the knees.

Thunder boomed long and low—warningly, it seemed to Joanna. But she had little time to dwell on that thought as she jogged along at Wade's side, feeling a bit in the way as a few Double L ranch hands scurried through the barn, latching most of the wooden windows and partially closing the sliding doors against more rain as it grew darker outside.

The first rattle of hail hit the big roof like a burst of gunfire.

"How's it look, Bill?" Wade shouted at the small, gnarled cowboy who came puffing through the west door.

"Ain't good," was the terse reply as the foreman glanced in Joanna's direction. An uncomfortable prickle of fear danced down her spine as she sensed suddenly that Bill was trying not to alarm her. "'Spose we can't do no more'n wait and see," he added.

"Let's not take any chances," Wade cautioned, and the other man nodded, then stepped outside again, skirting the rear of the barn and working his way from building to building as pea-sized hail continued to beat down.

"Nervous?"

Joanna glanced away from Bill's retreating back to look up into Wade's stern face. On the way over to the Double L, they'd heard on the radio the severe weather bulletin for their area. Wade hadn't seemed too concerned then, so Joanna had pushed her uncomfortable feelings aside. Until now.

"Yes, I guess I am," she admitted with a small shrug, then looked away. When a storm grew this bad in Iowa, she would have been listening to her weather radio, prepared to retreat to the basement of her apartment building. She'd seen too many news reports on television about the devastation wreaked by tornadoes not to feel apprehensive. Besides, Wade had given no indication that they would be taking cover anywhere, and Joanna's imagination was beginning to work overtime.

This storm was progressing like the ones meteorologists on television back in Iowa always warned viewers to watch for, she quickly realized. The huge, anvil-topped thunderheads that had built in the west in midafternoon had rolled toward the Double L relentlessly, their rapid increase and ominous approach tingeing the air an eerie yellow-green.

Shortly after she and Wade had driven over to the Double L, the wind had picked up. First had come the deluge of rain, and now hail. The next thing to watch for, according to what she'd learned, was the appearance of a wall cloud, a little extension of cloud emerging from the bottom of the thunderhead. And if the wall cloud began to rotate, and stretch toward the earth...

Joanna felt her cool fingers enveloped in the hard warmth of Wade's, and she unconsciously swayed nearer to him, unaware that she was clinging to his hand with surprising strength. When she turned her head to glance up at him, the sternness vanished from his face, and his eyes softened as he looked down at her and gave her hand a bracing squeeze. Joanna felt immeasurably better.

For several moments their gazes held, until finally Wade looked away to stare out into the near twilight beyond the barn doors. All at once the hail stopped and the storm grew quiet.

Suddenly Wade's hold on her hand tightened like a vise. "Let's turn 'em out!" he shouted to the ranch hands within hearing.

Joanna looked toward the storm, then gasped as she saw a dark funnel skim the ground, a spinning column of wind that was moving directly toward them from little more than a mile away. She was jerked around and found Wade's face level with hers, his lean fingers biting painfully into her upper arms.

"Get to the storm cellar south of the house," he ordered.

"W-what about you?"

"We're going to turn the stock out." He gave her a quick shove meant to send her on her way.

Joanna hesitated. "I think I should help."

"You'll just be in the way," Wade said as he ran to the nearest stall. Joanna hurried after him, dodging sideways when he emerged leading a horse. "Get out of here," he shouted, but Joanna held her ground.

"Tell me what I can do," she insisted, aware that they had little time to act before the tornado reached them.

"All right then, dammit. We need to get these horses turned out."

Joanna didn't wait, pivoting to run to the next stall. Grabbing a lead rope, she opened the stall door and looped the rope around the mare's neck as she'd seen Wade do, holding the loose ends together long enough to lead the animal outside the barn door and release her. But the mare balked just before Joanna could turn her out, fearful of leaving the security of her stall. Frustrated, Joanna pulled on the makeshift lasso, but it wasn't until Wade brought out another horse that the mare changed her mind and chased after her stablemate.

Fear lent Joanna strength and speed. The awful silence that had followed the hail was now building steadily to a roar that sounded like an oncoming freight train. Three other men worked with Joanna and Wade until every horse had been led from the barn. The rest of the hands were freeing stock from other buildings and smaller paddocks, driving the animals toward the open range in the hope that they would be able to flee the storm. Dirt and hay chaff from the barn floor clouded the air around them by the time they finished.

It was then that Joanna again looked toward the west and saw that the black, whirling column of wind, cutting a narrow path of violence directly toward the barn, was almost upon them. Astonished at the sight, she froze.

"Joanna!"

Wade's shout was almost lost in the rising howl, and Joanna turned and rushed toward him, her legs shaking so from raw fear that they felt like rubber. Wade grabbed her hand and together they ran toward the ranch house. Blinded by the airborne dirt and debris that stung her face, Joanna let Wade lead her, her heart nearly bursting with terror as she gripped her hat and used it to shield her eyes.

It seemed an eternity before they reached the storm cellar and Wade pulled the door open. Joanna stumbled down the stone steps, then fell to the earthen floor as Wade wrestled the door closed and barred it securely against the wild roar of wind that rattled it on its hinges.

"You all right?"

Joanna was just getting to her hands and knees from where she'd landed sprawled on the hard-packed floor, disoriented by the darkness. "Is there a lantern or something?" she asked as she gingerly got to her feet, closing her fingers slightly on her skinned, smarting palms as if to flex away some of the sting. She yelped in pain as she struck her head on the low ceiling.

"Be careful," Wade cautioned belatedly as she reached up to rub the tender spot on her scalp. His hand brushed her arm. "Stand still a minute." Joanna heard a snap, and a match tip flared to life, illuminating the small, cramped space. "We're damned lucky to have this to ourselves," he told her.

"It is small," she agreed, but was too grateful to be below ground to complain. "But what about the men?"

"There are two other cellars," Wade told her as he reached for the flashlight stashed in a cubbyhole in the wall and switched it on just before the match burned low. "I wasn't worried about sharing this with them. I meant that we're lucky we don't have to share it with any reptile friends. We're in rattlesnake country around here, you know."

Joanna shuddered. "I—I didn't think about that." She reached for the flashlight Wade held, placing her small hand over his to help guide the light toward every shadow and cobwebby crevice. In those few moments she completely forgot about the storm.

"If you're satisfied, I'd like to sit down." Wade didn't wait for her consent, but flashed the light once more around the small interior before he lowered himself to the earthen floor and leaned back against the wall, his long legs taking up much of the floor space. Joanna remained standing but stooped, not eager to sit down, even if there weren't any snakes.

Suddenly she was startled by a loud crash against the cellar door. Instinctively she flung herself at Wade. The flashlight clattered to the floor as Wade grabbed for her and pulled her downward. In an instant she was sitting between his thighs, enfolded in his long, strong arms. They stayed huddled together as the cellar door rattled dangerously on its hinges and lurched against the casing, until Joanna felt sure it would splinter.

Sand and grit showered through the small cracks in the door. Joanna turned her face into the shoulder of Wade's slicker, squeezing her eyes tightly shut. She gasped in alarm as the air seemed to resist going into her lungs, and her ears began to react uncomfortably to the changing air pressure.

"It's all right, honey," Wade murmured, holding her trembling form closer, wrapping his legs tightly around hers as if to envelop her in the rawhide toughness of his body. "It won't last much longer."

Joanna snuggled closer, her arms finding their way around Wade's neck. Outside, the sound of wood groaning and splintering punctuated the steady roar. They heard a giant crash—a veritable avalanche of sound that seemed to go on and on. It was just when the noise couldn't have got louder that the storm slowly moved on. The pressure in Joanna's ears immediately began to ease.

"Sounds like it's about over now. You all right?"

Wade's voice was soothing, reassuring, and Joanna realized that she loved the sound of that low, slightly husky drawl.

"Yes," she whispered as she lifted her head from Wade's neck, the light of the dropped flashlight just bright enough in the dusty air to enable her to see his face clearly. "Are you?"

Wade didn't answer right away, the delay making

her aware that her body was beginning to react to being held so securely. It didn't help that one of Wade's hands had somehow got beneath her slicker when he'd reached up to pull her down to him, and was now moving slowly up and down her back.

And all he had to do was touch her, she marveled. All it took was a touch, no matter how coincidental, to kindle that slow warm sweetness that was coursing through her veins and pooling deep inside. Being here in his arms with his hands on her in a subtly provocative way only multiplied those sensations, and Joanna knew she was in deep emotional danger.

Unfortunately for her Wade knew it, too, his gravelly sounding ''I'm fine'' managing to underscore the brusque way he reached behind his neck to pry her arms away. Joanna suddenly found herself lifted from between his thighs and set aside as he moved past her to open the cellar door.

Feeling Wade's rebuff deeply, she made a project of finding her hat until she could regain her composure. That he had little use for her was evident. She would have to try harder to remember that in the future, and stop succumbing to selective amnesia every time he came close to her.

Joanna got to her feet, wrestling with the yellow slicker that had tangled around her legs, careful to stoop low enough to avoid cracking her head on the ceiling again. Wade moved up the steps and braced his back against the cellar door to force it open. Joanna sensed the strain as he pushed upward, until the debris blocking the door at last began to shift, then slide away.

Once the door was open, Wade came back down the stairs to retrieve his hat and return the flashlight to the cubbyhole. As soon as there was room to do so, Joanna got past him and hurried out into the light rain that followed in the aftermath of the storm.

"Oh, no!" Joanna stifled the cry with a grimy hand, stunned at the destruction before her.

The house had sustained some damage, the pecan tree nearest it twisted and fallen, a large branch driven through the kitchen wall. Much of the roof had been stripped of shingles, and nearly every window on the west side of the house had been blown out.

But the main barn was the hardest hit, reduced to a pile of broken boards beneath the big roof that rested crookedly on one side of where the structure had stood. There was no way of telling how much feed and equipment might still be beneath it, since a good share of those things had ended up strewn across the corrals and into the open paddock opposite the house. She was now doubly thankful that they'd managed to get all the horses out before the tornado struck.

Joanna walked toward the devastation, then hurried past it, unable to see more than a few ranch hands until she'd almost reached the bunkhouse. A quick estimate of the number of men who were visible by then, scattered around inspecting the storm damage, assured her that nearly all had managed to reach shelter. To her relief, the two who at first appeared to be missing rode in from the range a few moments later, driving four horses ahead of them. By the time Joanna reached the corral where they'd put the horses, the pair had dismounted, and one was rolling a cigarette. Wade had caught up with her by then, too.

"Don't think we lost any of the horses," one of the men reported to Wade before he tipped the brim of his hat in deference to Joanna. "'Course we're goin' to have the devil's own time roundin' 'em up.'"

Wade nodded. "Do the best you can. We've got about three hours of daylight left. You'll have some help as soon as we find enough gear to get these horses saddled up."

"Sure thing." With that, both men remounted and rode off.

"What can I do, Wade?" Joanna was at a loss. Everywhere she looked there was something to be done. There didn't seem to be a building that hadn't sustained at least minor damage. The contents of the barn were strung over at least a quarter mile and needed to be taken out of the mud and rain. Tree limbs were scattered everywhere, as was the debris of the big barn. How they were going to find enough gear to saddle and bridle four horses in time to use them before nightfall was a mystery to her, since there was no way of knowing whether anything beneath the barn roof was accessible, or even usable.

"You can take care of the house," Wade was saying. "That's the toolshed." He gestured to a small building between the machine shop and storage shed. "Find yourself a hammer, some tacks and a roll of plastic, and get those windows covered. It would be best if you could cover them on the outside. Unless,'' he added as his gaze swung to meet hers, ''heights bother you. If they don't, you can help yourself to one of the ladders and get to work.''

And then he was off, striding toward the barn where a few of the men were already burrowing beneath the roof to salvage what they could. Two other men had a pickup truck in the pasture east of the house and were collecting what was there, while someone else was starting up a tractor. Everyone, it seemed, had found something to do without specific direction from Wade or Bill Black. Feeling oddly grateful to be assigned a part in the cleanup, Joanna stepped into the shed, assembled the items Wade had named and hurried to the house to do what she could.

It took her about an hour to cover all the windows but one with plastic. She was eager to start clearing away the broken glass inside. And yes, she was eager to look around the house itself, realizing from what she could see through the windows that it hadn't been lived in since she'd left Texas three years before. The furnishings were draped with sheets.

Joanna knocked the jagged row of glass out of the last window frame, the one in the kitchen, then climbed in through it. Once inside, she walked to the back door and unlocked it.

The kitchen had been showered with debris, and as with the other rooms she'd seen from outside, the floor was wet and needed mopping. Before she began to work, Joanna wandered through the house, a bit disappointed to see how woefully bland everything about it seemed to her now, its dingy paint and wallpaper in varied depressing shades of yellowed gray and tan.

The furniture beneath the sheets was still the same, functional but drab, and Joanna made a mental note to ask Wade if the Double L's bank account could stand the expense of an extensive remodeling job. Perhaps she'd need to purchase only a few new pieces of furniture to supplement what Wade had had shipped from her Des Moines apartment to Texas and stored. That would enable her to get rid of much of what was here.

The most important changes, however, could be wrought with a paintbrush, new wallpaper and good floor coverings, and Joanna was looking forward to getting started. She would be living here soon, and she intended to make the house as warm and comfortable a haven as her apartment had been.

It was nearly dark when she finished mopping up water and sweeping up glass. By then, two of the men had removed the huge branch from the hole in the kitchen wall and were nailing a big sheet of plywood over the opening. When they were through, Joanna locked the door and went off in search of something else to do.

By eleven that night she was exhausted. She had helped sort and drag what had been salvaged from the barn into the supply shed, as well as stack the pieces of wood that had been cut from the downed branches scattered all around the ranch headquarters. The electricity had been restored just before nightfall, enabling the work to continue long after dark. Having the power on so soon after a storm was nothing short of phenomenal, she'd been told.

And now she was working with Wade in one of the smaller barns, watching as he doctored a mare that had been badly cut on barbed wire. Gingerly Joanna gripped the twitch that had been applied to the mare's upper lip to both hold and distract the animal while Wade cleaned her wounds and applied antiseptic.

Of all her experiences with horses to date, this was the worst. Indeed, applying the contraption to the mare had seemed unnecessarily cruel, and she had refused to do it until Wade assured her that the mare would not be in pain. The fact that her initial resistance provoked him had been clear in his terse manner, and Joanna had dropped her objections, feeling just as ignorant as she was.

There was so much to learn—too much—and now that she was on the verge of exhaustion, her lack of knowledge where ranching was concerned seemed monumental. Even if she managed to somehow instantly acquire the knowledge, she would still be too inexperienced to use it competently. What bothered her most, she realized, was the thought that she'd never learn enough to gain anyone's respect, that she would always be an inept outsider who never quite fit in.

"All right, Joanna." Wade straightened and took the twitch from her. Slowly he untwisted the contraption, speaking gently to the mare as she was released.

As many as possible of the Double L horses were spending the night in corrals, the stalls being reserved for those that needed them most. Three horses that had charged through a barbed-wire fence during the storm that afternoon had been given priority stall space. The mare they'd just been with was the last to receive thorough attention, and Joanna was more than ready to call it a night when Wade finished settling the mare.

Tiredly she trailed behind Wade toward his pickup. That he even had a pickup that was usable was nothing short of miraculous, for the mighty wind had picked it up and carried it several feet from where it had been parked, finally dropping it on its side in the shallow ditch along the driveway. A heavy chain and a tractor had been needed to pull it upright, but apart from broken side mirrors and a large dent in one of the fenders, the silver-and-maroon vehicle was in one piece and still ran.

When they reached the truck, Wade opened the passenger door and Joanna climbed in, murmuring a quiet thank-you. To her surprise Wade started to get in after her, motioning her toward the driver's seat with a nod. Caught off guard, Joanna slid over.

"You can take us home tonight, Joanna," he said as he pulled off his hat and ran weary fingers through his black hair. "It's about time I let you do some of the driving."

Joanna's fatigue vanished as a feeling of dread hit her middle. Even in the best of moods, Wade would not have been pleased to discover she didn't know how to drive. But now that he was tired and, as far as she knew, still unhappy with her because she'd resisted his instructions with the mare, he was sure to be upset when she told him.

Wade expelled a long, tired breath and leaned his head back. "Let's go, Joanna."

Silence followed. In the illumination provided by the security light on the side of the machine shed, she looked at the buttons and gauges on the unfamiliar dashboard, and knew she'd never be able to bluff her way through this. She took a shallow breath before saying in a subdued voice, "I'm afraid you'll have to drive, Wade."

"Why? You too tired?"

She could have used that as an excuse, but it would have just been delaying the inevitable. "I am tired," she admitted quietly, then shrugged. Her lips stretched into a thin smile as she tried to force a touch of lightness into her voice, hoping Wade would take her confession better than she thought he would. "But the problem is that I've never learned to drive."

Her attempt to soften the words met with little success. Wade lifted his head to look across the seat at her. "Now why am I not surprised?" he remarked with weary sarcasm. "Maybe I should have you make a list of what you *do* know how to do. It's bound to be shorter than the list of things you don't know how to do."

Joanna wrenched open the truck door and stepped out, so frustrated and angry that all of her emotions seemed to be knotted in her chest and throat. She'd worked hard that day, harder after the storm, trying to compensate for her ignorance by making herself useful. She hadn't complained once about the work, the dirt, the mud or the fact that she'd been too busy to go to the dining hall for supper. She'd done everything Wade asked and several other things besides, conscious all the while of doing a good job so that no one would be able to find fault with her.

But all of it had escaped his notice. Nothing she'd done that day had earned her a particle of his respect. Oh, he hadn't lost his temper with her just now, but somehow, his sarcasm was worse. His remarks only served to underscore how futile he truly thought it was to try to teach her anything. Joanna felt her self-confidence shrivel as she walked around the front of the truck to the passenger side. Wade started the engine just as she stepped up into the cab and closed the door.

"I'm sorry, Joanna," he muttered.

Joanna didn't look in his direction, not acknowledging his apology in any way, afraid that she wouldn't be able to resist getting in a few caustic remarks of her own.

By the time they reached the highway, the steady hum of the truck tires on smooth pavement began to work on her like a lullaby, and she gradually slumped against the door and fell asleep. She stirred halfway to consciousness when they reached the Ten Star and Wade turned off the engine, got out and came to the passenger door.

Groggily she stumbled out of the truck, saved from

falling on her face when Wade caught her, then swept her into his arms. Sleep-dazed, she submitted easily, but halfway up the inside staircase from the kitchen, consciousness surged in, and she awoke with a jerk.

"Hold still," Wade grumbled as she stiffened in his arms and instinctvely clutched at his shoulders. The abrupt shift of her slight weight was enough to make him stop and sway to regain his balance.

"I can walk," she insisted as she struggled to get a foot on the next step.

"And I told you to hold still," he said sternly, flexing his arm to imprison her knees in its crook. "Falling down the stairs would be a fitting end to this day, but I'm not eager to add a broken back to the list of problems I've been collecting lately."

Joanna subsided immediately, knowing full well that she counted high on that list of problems.

"Now, put your arms around my neck and give me at least some help. You aren't heavy, but you are a handful."

Joanna did as he said, and Wade moved on up the stairs.

"I can walk," she reminded him again, wide-eyed and awake now, acutely aware of the faint scent of after-shave that still clung to his cheek and neck, a subtle accompaniment to the sweat, grime and horse odors that combined with something undeniably masculine and created what she considered a perverse appeal to her senses. It distressed her to realize that her attraction to Wade could be enhanced by something as common as dirt and sweat.

"So can I," he murmured, the lightly whiskered line of his jaw unrelenting as he reached the top of the stairs and walked along the hall to Joanna's door. Then, instead of setting her on her feet, Wade nudged open the door with the toe of his boot and carried her through the dark into her private bath.

"What was all that for?" she asked crossly once he put her down and snapped on the bathroom light. She had just turned away from him, when she caught sight of herself in the mirror and gasped.

"'All that' was because you're worn out," he told her as she reached up to touch her dirty, tangled hair, finger combing some of the looser snarls from its length, aghast that her face was just as grimy as her clothing. "And—" Wade reached out to turn her toward him and reclaim her full attention "—because I don't feel right about what I said to you."

Joanna withdrew from him slightly, self-conscious about the way she looked and uncomfortable with the sudden turn in conversation. "You were right," she said stiffly. "There isn't much I know how to do."

She took a quick breath as a thought suddenly occurred to her. She decided that in spite of the fact they both were exhausted, she would take advantage of this unexpected opportunity to get Wade to reconsider his agreement with her father. "And now that you realize you made a promise to my father that was impossible to keep—through no fault of yours," she was careful to add, "I hope you'll see sense and release us both from it. If you don't, I'm afraid we're going to have one unpleasant confrontation after another." She paused, edging farther away. "And I hate those."

Wade expelled a long breath and leaned back against the door frame. "I don't like them much myself. But that doesn't mean that I'm about to welsh on the agreement."

Joanna spun away, picking up the brush on the counter that skirted the sink and yanking it briskly through her hair. There was no talking to him when he used that hard tone of voice.

"That riles you, doesn't it?"

"What difference does it make how I feel?" she shot back.

"Sometimes feelings don't have a lot to do with it," he said quietly. "If I'm going to be an honorable man, I have to keep my word."

Joanna tugged the brush through her hair a couple more times, wishing she could find a way to convince him that some promises were impossible to fulfill—especially when one of the persons involved wanted no part of the agreement.

And that suddenly gave her an idea.

"What about contracts, Wade? When you sign your name, do you always honor every single detail?" she asked as she turned back to face him.

"Contracts, too," he assured her. "My name wouldn't be worth much around here if I didn't."

Joanna saw her chance and took it. "Then how do you rationalize breaking your word to me?" At Wade's surprised look, she went on, "I'm not certain if a marriage certificate is a contract or not, but isn't a verbal consent to love, honor and cherish before signing your name the same as giving your word?''

Wade's expression darkened so quickly that Joanna's bravado wavered, but she continued anyway. ''S-so I think you can see the point I'm trying to make. Since you feel no qualms of conscience about our getting a divorce, I don't think amending your agreement with my father should bother you much. Unless, of course,'' she put in with faint bitterness, ''your word means less when you give it to me than it does when you give it to someone else.''

By the time she finished talking Wade was no longer leaning against the door frame but was towering over her, his face an iron mask, his eyes blazing with anger and frustration. ''Dammit all, if you don't have a way of putting the wrong twist on everything!''

''It's not a wrong twist,'' she insisted incautiously. ''It's just another of your double standards.''

''Another?'' His voice had gone quiet, the silky drawl conveying his displeasure far more effectively than sharp words. But Joanna was just tired enough and cross enough to go on.

''Like your love for Lorna and my friendship with Jake. You feel free to pursue Lorna while still married to me, but heaven help me if I have a male friend while I'm married to you.''

''I thought we settled that,'' he growled.

''You probably thought so, once you'd criticized me for my innocent friendship with Jake. But you're getting away from the subject,'' she injected hastily.

"I'm trying to convince you to forget about that agreement. I know you mean well, but it just won't work. If Bill Black wouldn't mind having me watch over his shoulder for the next few years, you could go ahead and release us all—you, me *and* Lorna—from this now, before one of us gets ulcers."

Wade studied her gravely for several moments. "I've given it a lot of thought," he admitted. "I won't tell you I haven't. But that was before I began to realize how much you really do need my help."

"Why?" Joanna demanded. "Because you found out I can't drive a car?"

"It's not just that."

"I think you're overreacting," she said dismissively. "Not learning how to ride a horse or drive a car by twenty-one isn't the tragedy you seem to think it is. Not everyone was raised like you and Megan."

"I realize that, too, Joanna," he said patiently. "But there aren't many people who come into a big ranching operation like the Double L with so little basic knowledge."

"I don't need—"

"You *do* need," he cut in harshly. "That damned agreement has nothing to do with my motives for seeing you through this now. You need me, and we're not going to argue about this again. Either you settle down and behave a little more like that gentle, soft-spoken girl you were when I married you, or you and I are going to raise some dust."

Joanna's eyes widened. "Then we'll just have to raise some dust," she hissed, outraged at his words.

"Not for anything in the world am I going to revert into that meek, miserable little mouse that nobody wanted to have around! No one is ever going to hurt and manipulate me like that again!"

Joanna was shaking now, shaking with the sudden eruption of a lifetime of emotions, betraying herself to Wade in a way that brought first open surprise, then a frown of concern to his tanned, lightly weathered face. When she realized what she'd said, she pressed her lips tightly closed, her posture going rigid as she brought herself under severe control.

"Joanna…" Wade's voice was low, conciliatory as he reached for her.

Joanna took a step back to avoid his touch, even as she felt everything in her cry out to be held. "I—I'm sorry," she murmured, her throat dry. "I'm guess I'm just tired. Please leave me alone. I want to be alone."

"I'm the one who's sorry, Joanna. And I don't think I want to leave you just now." There was a tenderness in his voice that served only to weaken her precarious control over the fountain of tears she was trying to keep back.

"You have to go," she said crossly. "Right now I just want to take a quick shower and get in bed. I don't feel like arguing with you half the night." Cloaking her vulnerability in irritation, Joanna managed to drive away the sting of tears and regain her composure. But Wade merely stared down at her, curiosity and perception mingling in the intent way he looked at her. Then his expression changed and she felt her tension begin to recede.

"I think you impressed the boys over at the Double L tonight," he said at last, surprising her with the abrupt change of subject. "I don't reckon any of us expected to see you pitch in like that, when a lot of city women would have been afraid of breaking a nail or getting dirty. It made me kind of proud."

Now it was Joanna's turn to stare.

Then suddenly he was leaning toward her, touching his lips to hers before she realized what had happened. It was a fleeting contact, but when he withdrew, he lingered a moment an inch or so away as if seriously considering kissing her again.

"Don't bother getting up in the morning until you feel rested," he told her. And then he was gone, leaving the small, still room and unknowingly taking a good bit of her heart with him.

CHAPTER SIX

THE NEXT FEW DAYS were different from any Joanna had known yet on the Ten Star. Something had changed for the better in her relationship with Wade, but she would have been hard put to pinpoint just what. He was still his stern self, polite yet taciturn, often irritable, but at the same time he seemed just a little more apt to compliment her, or say something to put her at ease. He seemed less like her father all the time.

At first, she'd thought her outburst the night of the storm had evoked his pity, influencing the subtle change between them, but the time or two she managed to send his temper sky-rocketing quickly assured her that pity had no part in their relationship.

She'd gradually grown more relaxed with him, and the more she relaxed, the easier it was to be patient with herself and the great number of things she had yet to learn. To her surprise, she was beginning to feel she might not always have to rely on a foreman to run the Double L, after all. Wade's occasional word of encouragement helped her to feel there was no reason to lag back and let someone else make all the decisions and give all the orders.

Unfortunately the positive changes between them were having an effect on Joanna's emotions. The fact that they spent hours on end alone together seemed to enhance the growing sense of companionship between them, and the attraction she felt toward Wade was growing perilously intense. When she added to that the fact that he was legally her husband, Joanna knew she was in danger of falling just a bit in love with him.

"Do you suppose it would be all right for me to use some of the insurance money for the house to make a few changes in the part of the kitchen that was damaged?" she asked him early one afternoon as they were going over the Double L books.

"What kind of changes?" he asked, not looking up from the ledger he was working on.

"I was thinking that instead of repairing the hole in the wall, it would be nice to put in sliding glass doors and lay some stone for a patio there. I'd still want to keep the side door for convenience, but a patio door would let in a lot more light and air and make the kitchen a more pleasant place to work and eat."

She had Wade's full attention now.

"What you're talking about could cost more than the insurance will pay."

"Then I'd settle for putting in the patio door for now," she said, shrugging to hide her disappointment. "The patio could come later." After a moment's thought she asked, "What about the cost of replacing the barn? Was it insured for enough to build a new barn of the same size?''

"I updated the coverage on all the buildings just last year, but since you have to rebuild the main barn, I'd like to see you build something bigger." Wade was leaning back in his chair, looking at her over strong interlaced fingers.

"Can I afford to do that?"

Wade smiled. "Maybe we should see if you can figure out the answer to that question."

"Me?"

"Why not? You'll be faced with problems like this more often than you think. It's a good way for you to learn how to manage ranch finances. Go ahead and take the rest of the afternoon to look over the books. Pay attention to ranch income from the past three years, and see if you can project what you'll have this year after expenses. And don't forget to check market prices. Try to come up with an answer based solely on this year's profits—not counting Double L savings and investments—and we'll talk about it after dinner tonight."

"I don't think I'm ready for this," she remarked doubtfully.

"You may not be," Wade agreed, "but whether you are or not, you'll learn more in an afternoon of trying to answer your own question than you will if I give you an easy answer now." He leaned forward, resting his forearms on the desk. "You'll find the ledgers you need on the bottom shelf of the far cabinet." He nodded toward the section of cabinets beneath the bookshelves that lined one wall. "You can look over this one when I'm finished with it," he added before he once again became absorbed in what he'd been doing.

The afternoon passed quickly as Joanna leafed through page after page of figures, often distracted from her main objective by the frequent questions that came to mind. Consuelo called them to dinner just as she finished with the current year's ledger and completed what she considered amateurish calculations of what the Double L could afford.

Dinner went as usual, with Megan supplying most of the conversation. This evening's topics were the barbecue at a neighboring ranch on Saturday night and the complete unsuitability of what now hung in Megan's closet.

Joanna listened as brother and sister discussed the outing that she and Wade had quarreled over the night Jake and Lorna came to the Ten Star for dinner. At first, she was surprised to realize that she had forgotten about the barbecue that was now only three days away—until she also recalled that Wade had clearly expressed his desire for her to stay home that night. Since she would not be attending, she had put it out of her mind, determined not to give way to either resentment or self-pity.

"And what about you, Joanna?" Wade asked her in mock exasperation. "Are you suddenly going to decide that what you bought in San Antonio won't do Saturday night?"

Joanna looked up, startled. Quietly she answered,

"I wasn't planning to go." There was a moment's silence before Wade's eyes went hard, as if he'd just remembered their quarrel. The almost frivolous atmosphere that had dominated the dinner discussion was abruptly stifled.

"Then you'd better change your plans."

Joanna's eyes started to waver from his, then stubbornly maintained contact. No matter what he was hinting at, he didn't really want her to go, and this unexpected bit of pretense was confusing and upsetting for her. "I'd rather not."

Wade's lips twisted. "Nothing's ever simple with you, is it?"

Joanna wiped her mouth with her napkin, angry and a little hurt at the wealth of irritation Wade's remark had given away. It was obvious to her now that the change for the better in their relationship had been either a product of wishful thinking or was too frail to withstand all but the most minor stress.

"All the more reason for me to stay home," she told him, then suddenly realized he could be looking for a graceful way out of being expected to take her to the barbecue. A refusal, coupled with the right words from her, would absolve him of any guilty feelings he might have been bothered by in the past few days. Whether he'd consciously intended it or not, this well-timed little dinner discussion was the perfect out for them both. Who would expect him to take his wife anyplace if she flatly refused to go? "After all," she went on, confident now that she understood what was really going on, "you and I hardly have the kind of relationship either of us wants paraded before your neighbors.''

''That's for sure,'' Megan remarked sarcastically.

''Stay out of this, Meg,'' Wade ordered.

The harsh, angry look on his face gave Joanna a feeling of uncertainty. Hadn't she taken her cue and done what he wanted? she wondered.

''How can I stay out of it?'' Megan argued. ''I'm not wild about her going, either. Somehow I can't picture introducing her to all our friends. I was shamed enough when you decided you had to marry her.''

''Megan…'' Wade growled warningly as Joanna tossed down her napkin next to her plate and pushed back her chair to stand.

''But not quite shamed enough to refrain from using my inheritance to regain your own,'' Joanna pointed out, feeling some satisfaction at the way Megan's scornful gaze suddenly dropped. ''Your gratitude for what my money provided for you has been overwhelming, Megan. But it's a bit late for contrition now, don't you think?'' She looked down at Megan's bent head. ''Besides, I can't say I'm too thrilled to be a member of this family, either. And I intend to spare all of us the public embarrassment of being seen together.''

With that, Joanna stalked from the room and retreated to the den, shaking with anger as she just managed to keep from slamming the door. Darn Megan! She'd had enough of her spite and sarcasm.

Yet on the other hand, she wasn't very proud of

herself for having thrown the Hollisters' desperation for money three years ago into their faces. Never one to be cruel, Joanna's anger slowly chilled into a queasy feeling of remorse.

What was happening to her these days? Wade had brought her back to Texas just five weeks ago, but already she had changed from the reserved young woman she had been into a quarrelsome, outspoken stranger. She'd always endured life's pains and frustrations in silence, and scarcely knew what to think of herself now.

One thing was becoming clear: she couldn't tolerate being manipulated and ordered about now any more than she'd been able to three years before. And after this little run-in with Megan, she guessed she'd put up with one too many insults from the other woman to just go on enduring them in silence.

Joanna continued to fret over her remarks at the dinner table until Consuelo interrupted her by bringing in a small insulated coffee server on a tray.

"This was very thoughtful of you, Consuelo," she said as she took the tray from her and placed it on the desk, taking special note of the fact that Consuelo had brought only one cup. "Won't Mr. Hollister be doing paperwork tonight?"

"I think not, *señora*. He has gone." Consuelo couldn't quite meet her gaze and started to turn away to bustle out of the room.

"Did he say where he was going?" she asked before Consuelo got very far. It was clear that the woman was uncomfortable with her, and that only increased Joanna's sense of guilt about what she'd said at the dinner table. It was possible that Consuelo had overheard, even though Joanna knew the woman wasn't one to deliberately eavesdrop.

"He has gone to the Kemp ranch, *señora*. He did not say when he would be back," she added, anticipating Joanna's next question.

"And what about Megan?" Joanna ventured, thinking she should probably apologize to her.

"She went out for the evening. I do not know where."

"Thank you," Joanna murmured as Consuelo left the den and closed the door softly.

So Wade was on his way to the Kemp ranch to see Lorna. Joanna felt her low spirits sag further. He hadn't seen Lorna for days, and Joanna had foolishly hoped that the woman's hold on him was not as strong as she'd first thought.

But she'd been wrong, she concluded sadly as she poured herself a cup of coffee and walked around the desk to make herself comfortable in Wade's big chair. She sat there for some time before a new thought had her reaching for the Double L ledgers she'd been bent over most of the afternoon.

She leafed through them again with renewed purpose, this time figuring how much more money it would take to cover the cost of all the decorating changes she'd been mulling over for the ranch house. Added to that was a rough estimate of whether or not she could afford a monthly payment on a car once she learned to drive and got her license. And that brought to mind the necessity of hiring a driving instructor, which included the expense of either bringing the instructor out to the ranch, or paying someone to drive her into town for lessons.

Joanna sighed, finally closing the ledgers and stacking them, along with her tablet of figures, on a corner of the desk. Noticing that her coffee had gone cold, she took the tray to the kitchen and grabbed her light jacket from the peg.

"I'm going for a walk, Consuelo," she told the housekeeper, who was just finishing up in the kitchen. At the woman's nod of acknowledgment, Joanna stepped out the door.

The night was cooler than she'd expected, and that only seemed to add to the mild melancholy that had gradually colored her every thought. Not even the beauty of the star-strewn Texas sky seemed to have much effect on her somber mood. Joanna strolled slowly along, realizing that, aside from her feelings of guilt about her bad behavior at supper, she was depressed about the isolation of the Ten Star.

Perhaps it would be different when she learned to drive and could come and go as she pleased. Being without a car in Des Moines had been inconvenient, but with buses and cabs she'd never felt stranded. Out here, where the only transportation was a car or a pickup or a horse, your mobility was definitely limited if you didn't know how to drive.

Joanna sighed, recognizing the beginnings of the deep, black loneliness she hadn't felt in ages. Linked to it was a sudden awareness: she didn't want to be divorced from Wade. What she truly wanted was for Wade to fall in love with her and forget all about Lorna Kemp.

And that wasn't possible. If it was going to happen, it would have happened before now, and Wade would be here with her tonight instead of at Lorna's.

Joanna had just turned around to head back when she heard a car pull up to the main house. Not especially eager to face either Wade or Megan now, she hung back for a while, then finally wandered over to pat the pair of friendly horses that had stepped up to the corral fence to thrust their long muzzles in her direction.

"Is that you, Lucky?" Joanna asked a shadowy face. She could just make out the wide blaze in the dim starlight, for the security light that shone over the barn left the spot where they were standing in near darkness. As if to answer her, the large nose nudged her affectionately. "And who's your buddy?" she asked as she rubbed the much lighter-colored horse that was nibbling at the hem of her jacket.

"Joanna?"

Startled, Joanna turned her head in time to see Jake Terrell step into a column of light just a few feet away.

"Consuelo said you'd gone for a walk," he said as he came toward her. "Want some company?"

Joanna smiled at the sound of Jake's slow Texas drawl. "I'd love some company," she told him, feeling her melancholy ease.

"Wade and Megan around?"

Joanna gave both horses an extra pat. "No. They're gone for the evening," she said with forced brightness. "Wade's at Lorna's, and I don't know where Megan is."

"You should have gone along with Wade. Lorna's been hoping you'd find time to stop over and visit her," Jake remarked. "It can get mighty lonely out here sometimes."

Joanna shrugged, not wanting to admit that going with Wade to Lorna's had not been an option, since he hadn't invited her, much less bothered to inform her that he was going anywhere. Jake took a pack of cigarettes from his pocket and shook one out. Neither spoke until Jake had the cigarette lit.

"What brings you to the Ten Star?" she asked, eager to make conversation once she sensed he was in no real hurry to leave.

"Hadn't been around to see you for a spell, and decided to see how you were coming along," he said, his mouth quirking into a smile. "Heard you had a little wind over at the Double L."

Joanna laughed at the understatement. "We certainly did. No one was hurt and we didn't lose any livestock, but I guess it will be a while before the insurance company settles the claim so I can replace the barn."

Jake nodded. "Funny how they want their premiums paid on time, but when you want them to hurry up and get your claim settled, it's a different story." Jake paused to take a quick drag on his cigarette.

"You and Wade going to the shindig over at the Cliburns' place Saturday night?"

Suddenly uncomfortable, Joanna stepped away from the fence and started walking slowly toward the house. Jake fell into step beside her, hooking a thumb in his belt, his loose-jointed swagger giving him a lazy, unhurried appearance.

"Are you?" she stalled.

"Yep."

They walked on for quite a ways, and Joanna thought she'd managed to get out of giving a direct answer until Jake spoke again.

"Never did hear you say whether you and Wade were going Saturday night."

Joanna shrugged, glancing toward Jake, just able to see his half smile beneath the shadow of his hat brim in the gray light of the ranch yard.

"I don't really want to go, Jake," she murmured as she looked away, embarrassed to tell him the whole truth—that Wade, and especially Megan, didn't want her to go to the barbecue, either.

Joanna was mildly surprised when Jake's next step brought him closer and he slipped his arm around her waist to pull her against his side. Her arm automatically went around his waist as his stride matched itself to hers.

"You aren't thinking of hiding yourself from everybody out here, are you, honey?" The big hand tightened promptly on her waist urged her to answer.

"I don't know."

Jake took another long, thoughtful draw on his cigarette and exhaled slowly. "I think I've got a fair idea of what's wrong," he said before he flicked his cigarette into the dirt just ahead of them, then stepped on it without breaking their slow stride. It was a moment before he spoke again. "But no matter what happens with you and Wade, you're going to be living here. You need to get out and meet people."

Joanna couldn't look at Jake. "You know about my...marriage to Wade?" she asked softly, not certain if he knew all the details, but reasoning from what he'd just said that he'd guessed. After all, Wade Hollister wouldn't have come near a seventeen-year-old girl for love, not when he could have had Lorna.

"I've known about it from the first," he admitted grimly, disapproval coloring his deep drawl.

"Then I think you can understand how awkward it would be if I went with Wade Saturday night," she said stiffly, not wanting to discuss it further. Jake was too easy to confide in.

"Could be awkward," he allowed. "On the other hand, you might have a good time."

Joanna found herself wishing that were true, but said nothing and shrugged, glad they had almost reached the stone patio at the back of the main house.

"This is where I'd better say adios," Jake said as they crossed the stones and he reached to open the door for her. "How 'bout saving me a dance Saturday night?"

"I never learned how to dance," she replied, not

bothering to repeat that she'd not likely be going to the barbecue.

"That's easily remedied, Joanna. Good night."

"Good night," she called after him, watching him disappear into the shadows.

She was just closing the inside door and turning around, when she saw Wade.

Guilt brought her gaze to the floor and flooded her cheeks with color as she turned to slip out of her light jacket and hang it on a peg. Then she reminded herself that she had no reason to feel guilty. "I didn't hear you drive in."

"I guess not," he said gruffly, as good as telling her outright that he'd seen her with Jake.

"How's Lorna?" she parried lightly, subtly challenging his disapproval of her being with Jake, when he'd spent the evening at the Kemp ranch with Lorna.

"Lorna's doing fine."

Joanna didn't look at him directly as she started for the stairs. After the incident at dinner and her long walk, she was more than ready for a relaxing soak in the tub and a good night's sleep. If she could manage to end the evening without having to endure a confrontation with Wade, all the better.

"If you're not too tired," Wade said, "I'd like to go over those figures on the barn."

To her surprise, his gruff voice had mellowed, and she flashed a quick, assessing look at his face. The steely glimmer in his eyes almost made her refuse, but another part of her reasoned that cooperating with him was likely the only way to smooth over the situation. She still had too much to learn, too much time left with him to allow any avoidable antagonism to prolong it. She nodded and followed him to the den.

"What's all this?" he asked as he picked up the tablet. His brows knit closely as he scanned the top sheet of figures, then leafed through the next two pages, easily reading her small, neat handwriting.

"I was trying to estimate how much money I'd need to do some remodeling on the ranch house," she explained as he sat on the front edge of the desk and stretched his long legs out before him, crossing them at the ankles. "And I didn't think it would be a good idea to tie up any Double L vehicles for my personal use, so I also figured in monthly payments on a car."

Wade grunted. "I see you've included driving lessons." His impatient gaze sped over the pages before he tossed the tablet onto his desk and folded his arms over his chest. "You came up with all this after supper tonight?" His blue eyes lanced into hers.

"Yes."

Wade ran lean fingers through his hair in a delaying gesture, his well-chiseled features slackening. He motioned her toward the leather sofa before the wall of bookshelves.

"Sit down, Joanna. Please," he added, the word softening the harsh sound of his voice. Wade seemed uncharacteristically ill at ease, and she went over and sat quietly at the near end of the sofa, wary yet curious.

"I apologize for what was said tonight," he began gravely. "Neither Megan nor I have ever treated you

very fairly, or expressed our gratitude very well.''
Wade paused, as if weighing what he should say next.
"A lot of it has to do with our shock over Chad's
sudden death in the plane crash and the magnitude of
what we later discovered he'd done. Those were painful times for us, and I'm afraid that having you here
now has been more of a reminder of that time than
either Megan or I expected.''

Joanna stared down at the clasped hands in her lap
for several moments. It seemed she had never been
someone whose presence was associated with happiness and good times. She remembered well how hard
it had been after her mother's death when her father
sent her away to live with her aunt. She would never
forget the disappointment on her aunt's face when
she'd first laid eyes on her, obviously expecting a
pretty child who favored her mother, getting instead
a somber girl who, in spite of Joanna's best efforts,
had managed to get on her nerves far too frequently
for either of them to be happy. Her father's reception
of her homecoming hadn't made it a happy one, either, and he'd always seemed to go out of his way to
avoid spending time with her.

Joanna would have been surprised to discover that
the deep glimmers of sadness in her hazel eyes revealed to her husband so much of what she was thinking and feeling. Somewhere along the line, she had
lost some of her ability to retreat behind a facade of
aloof reserve.

"It's too bad the two of you never associated me
with providing a way for you to save the Ten Star,''

she said then. "But I expect you credit my father with that," she concluded in a quiet voice, which bore only faint traces of her unhappiness.

"I was merely explaining the reason, Joanna," he went on. "I wasn't trying to excuse the reception you've got from us."

Joanna's mouth formed a grim line. "I believe what you've said is true in your case," she said slowly. "Especially since you were the one who was hurt the most by the desperate measures you felt forced to take. But I doubt it's true for Megan," she got in, not really caring if her words riled him. "She behaved like this long before your brother died."

Wade raised a big hand and wearily rubbed the back of his neck, surprising her with his benign reaction. "Megan's been a handful ever since our mother died and she grew up knowing she was the apple of her daddy's eye. We all spoiled her, encouraged her precociousness, and bragged about her sass. I don't think any of us gave a thought to the day when the chickens would come home to roost."

Joanna sensed, by the fond look that had come into his eyes despite what he was saying, that Wade was recollecting some incident concerning Megan that had, no doubt, endeared her even more to her father and brothers. It had probably been easy for a bright, pretty little girl growing up in a household of men to be overindulged and to develop a few arrogant attitudes about the world and her place in it. But Joanna was still too aware of her own bleak childhood to feel tolerant of a child who'd had every material advantage plus the almost worshipful love of her father and brothers, yet had turned out as spiteful and self-centered as Megan had.

"If that's all you have to tell me, I'd like to get to bed," she said briskly as she rose to her feet.

"No, that's not all," he said as he seemed to come out of the memory. "I wanted to talk to you about next Saturday night."

Joanna's eyes darted from his, and she took a step nearer the door, not wanting to hear what he would say. He had just explained that no matter how grateful he felt toward her, she was still an unpleasant reminder of a time he'd rather forget. Besides, she'd done her part at dinner by getting him off the hook so he could go to the Cliburn barbecue and have a good time, perhaps with Lorna, and she really didn't care to hear any more about it.

"There's nothing left to talk about," she said stiffly.

"There's a lot left to talk about," he argued. "And I plan to keep on talking until you agree to go."

Joanna looked over at him, surprised. "But you don't want me to go," she reminded him.

"When did I ever say that?" he shot back, his eyes sparking with temper.

"I don't think you ever said so...not in so many words," she answered. "But you made it clear."

Wade shook his head. "You're the only one who's been opposed to the idea."

"That's not true. The night Jake and Lorna came

over, you deliberately misunderstood my friendship
with Jake and—''

"And you drew the wrong conclusion," he cut in.
"But that's probably my fault for not handling it
right.''

"I've never expected to go, Wade. In fact—" she
released a quick breath "—I don't even want to.''
She turned to make a fast escape. "I'd like to get to
bed now. Good night.''

"Not yet, Joanna," he said, the iron in his voice
compelling her to stay where she was. "Come back
here."

Hesitantly Joanna turned, then stepped closer, her
eyes moving over his half-sitting, half-standing posture before she could catch herself. At six four he
normally towered over her, but perched as he was on
the edge of his desk with his long legs stretched out
before him, his face was level with hers. When she
was within a few inches of him, he uncrossed his arms
and reached for her hand, tugging her so close to his
side that her left thigh brushed his momentarily.

"I'm asking you to go with me," he said, his voice
oddly gentle, its low, rough timbre wrapping com-
fortingly around the old hurts their conversation had
stirred to life.

Joanna tugged her hand away and shook her head,
not looking at him as she moved a comfortable distance away. "That's not possible.''

"And why not?" he challenged in that same low,
rough drawl.

"How would we even behave?" she asked, not realizing until this moment how frightened she was of going into a crowd of strangers under these circumstances. "We barely know each other, and what we do know, neither of us likes. Everyone there will be able to tell how shaky our relationship is."

"How will they be able to do that?" he demanded softly.

Joanna shrugged and chafed a nervous palm against the denim of her jeans. It was a moment before she could answer. "A man and woman in love have learned things about each other that neither of us have a notion about. W-we don't even feel married," she said a little desperately as she felt the warm male aura of his body cascading over hers, helpless as a deep part of her began to respond.

"What do you suggest? That we pretend we're in love?" the softness was ebbing from his voice.

"Is that what you think we should do?" she countered and chanced a look at him.

Wade's voice dropped to a half growl, half grunt. "That's the last thing I want."

Joanna blinked away the sudden sting of tears, her lips thinning obstinately. "I won't go if you're planning to use the occasion to reveal to everyone how imminent our divorce is." Not that they wouldn't be able to tell by looking, she added to herself.

"I wouldn't do that," he muttered darkly.

"Maybe not intentionally," she allowed. "But what about Megan?" Joanna wasn't eager to expose herself to Megan's rapier tongue in front of a crowd of the other woman's friends.

''Megan's already given me her word that she'll be on her best behavior.''

Joanna looked away, not knowing if she should trust Megan. It wasn't unreasonable to think that Megan could still find some way to cause her an excruciatingly awkward moment or two. Still, if Megan had given Wade her word, wouldn't she keep it? Joanna might mean nothing to her, but Wade did. Surely that would be enough.

''All right,'' she said at last, her shoulders sagging a bit as she gave in.

''You're going to a barbecue, Joanna,'' Wade reminded her chidingly. ''It's supposed to be something you look forward to.''

''Not for me,'' she said, her mind filling with pictures of Wade virtually abandoning her in a crowd of strangers while he spent all his time at Lorna's side.

''Then start looking forward to it,'' he advised. ''The Cliburns always throw a good party.''

Joanna nodded and murmured something appropriate before she said good-night and left to go to her room. She had no doubt that what Wade had said about the Cliburns' parties was true. She only hoped that this particular one would be no different.

CHAPTER SEVEN

FRUSTRATED, JOANNA PULLED the curved, ornamental comb from her honey-streaked hair, tossing it down in disgust. She grabbed up her brush and ran it briskly through the unruly cascade of loose curls that refused to be confined.

For nearly two hours now, she'd been getting ready for the barbecue—washing her hair, taking a bath, applying her makeup. Finished except for her lipstick and dress, she had been trying to arrange her hair into a more restrained style—to no avail. Then a swift glance at her alarm clock had told her time was running out. She had just laid aside the brush and removed her dress from the closet, when a sharp knock sounded on her bedroom door.

"Just a minute," she called, tugging the topaz dress over her head and pulling it down over her slip. The knock came again as she rapidly worked at the tiny buttons down the front of the bodice, sighing in frustration as her fingers fumbled. She called out a harried "Come in" as she finished the task. The door swung open just as she smoothed the skirt of the dress into place.

Wade stood in the doorway, looking slightly

stunned as his eyes passed over the V-necked dress, lingering momentarily on the bodice buttons before passing over her snugly fitted waist and sweeping down the soft gathers of the skirt to her legs. He spared her nylon-clad feet a second's glance before his eyes made a slow return to her flushed cheeks.

For several heartbeats of time he stood there, slack jawed, as he took in the riotous disarray of her hair. He looked for all the world as if he was trying to think of a tactful comment, she was certain. It was when he seemed about to say something that she spoke instead.

"My apologies," she said with quiet dignity. "This is the best I can do." With that, she turned away and crossed the room to her bathroom, leaving the door open as she selected a tube of lipstick in a soft shade, and picked up a lipstick brush to draw a careful outline of her lips. Before she could start, Wade's reflection joined hers as he leaned against the doorjamb to watch.

"Who's complaining?" he asked as he let his eyes wander down the back of her, taking special note of her femininely rounded backside as she leaned forward a bit to begin to brush on her lipstick. "I was just thinking that I'm going to be the envy of every man in this part of Texas tonight."

Joanna blushed, but kept quiet, not knowing how to take the compliment. Although she knew she was no longer the plain child she once had been, she wasn't sure if she was any more than marginally attractive. She'd received too few compliments on her appearance to know whether Wade's was genuine or not.

He was so handsome. Tall and dark, he had eyes so vividly blue they were a magnet for her own. He was wearing a chocolate-brown leather Winchester vest over a blue shirt that enhanced the color of his eyes. Instead of a string tie he had opted to leave his shirt unbuttoned halfway to his silver-buckled waist, revealing a tantalizing view of hair-roughened male chest. Brown dress slacks unashamedly hugged his lean hips and muscular thighs, and he had selected a pair of highly polished black boots to complete the Western look that for him was as natural as taking a breath. Joanna couldn't help but stare until those wandering blue eyes leapt up suddenly to catch hers.

Something significant was happening between them. She sensed it in the sexy way he was leaning against the doorjamb and in the way he couldn't seem to keep his eyes from her.

"You look…handsome," she said shyly, then shifted her gaze to stare determinedly at the line she was trying to draw on her lips as she felt heat creep higher in her cheeks. "Did you want something? I need to finish getting ready." *And I can't do it with you standing there watching every move I make,* she added silently. The small room was suddenly too warm. Her pulse beat erratically.

"What I came in here for can wait. Go ahead with what you're doing," he said, his eyes fixed intently on her mouth. "I don't get to see many women fuss over themselves."

"I think you've been looking at too many cows lately," she murmured dryly as she tightened her lips to finish the outline, then used the lipstick tube to fill them in.

"You could be right. Seems like I'm just plain hungry for some soft, pretty sights," he drawled, letting his eyes roam over the reflection of her face before they dropped to her back and moved slowly downward.

"Shouldn't you be saying that kind of thing to Lorna?" she asked, unnerved by the way he was talking to her, scared of how easy it might be for her to believe it. She could easily fall in love with Wade, and any further show of sexual interest from him was likely to draw her over the edge to disaster. "Unless you were just practicing on me," she added, the lightness in her voice masking her fear that he was doing just that.

Being married to Wade and living on the Ten Star had been working on her emotions for weeks now; their daily closeness and the frequent moments of sexual awareness between them had combined to present a potentially volatile emotional situation. And now that he was in her room, watching her prepare for the evening while he made a few lazily suggestive remarks, she didn't think she could quite handle the staggering effect it all was having on her.

Wade's smiling, relaxed expression hardened slightly. "Jealousy doesn't become you, Joanna."

Her eyes fled his as she finished with her makeup and pushed the tube of lipstick into her small handbag, along with a comb and compact. Feeling unpleasantly self-conscious, she reached for her brush to try one last time to arrange her hair into the upsweep she'd intended.

"It looked better the way you had it," Wade commented when she finished, the glittering warmth in his eyes doing odd things to her insides. Now that she could see the result of her efforts, Joanna had to admit he was right. The one-sided upsweep looked all right, but her hair looked more attractive worn loose. Holding back an exasperated sigh, she gave the ornamental comb a tug, releasing the silken fall of curls before going at them again with her brush.

"Easy with that," Wade said as he stepped forward and, surprisingly, took the brush from her. Then he was threading his long, tanned fingers through her hair, fluffing it up until it fairly bounced with curling vitality. Too dazed by the explosion of sensation he was creating, Joanna was unaware of the slightly out-of-focus look she was giving his reflection.

"Look at yourself," he commanded gently, his firm lips curved into a bone-melting smile. Struggling to regain her composure, Joanna forced her eyes away from his and did as he said. What she saw stunned her.

Large hazel eyes, the green in them turned almost to molten gold by the topaz dress, stared at her out of a delicately shaped face. Smooth fair skin, enhanced by the light touch of cosmetics, glowed appealingly, the soft shade of lipstick drawing attention from her eyes to the innocent sensuality of her parted lips. But it was her hair, which she had always thought oddly colored, with its carefree disarray of what now looked to be sun-streaked curls, that provided the fitting frame for the late-blooming loveliness of her face.

"Like I said," Wade murmured close to her ear, "I'm going to be the envy of every man in this part of Texas."

Joanna couldn't suppress the thrill of pleasure that surged through her, or the shy smile that touched her lips.

"I brought you a little something," he said then as he slipped a hand inside his vest and withdrew a slender jeweler's box. Still standing behind her, he reached around to hold the box in front of her as she raised timid fingers to take it. The hinged lip opened smoothly, and Joanna gave a soft gasp.

Inside was a small, partially opened gold rosebud on a serpentine chain so fine it looked to be no more than tightly twined golden cobwebs.

"When Megan and I flew into San Antonio yesterday, I came across this."

"It's beautiful, Wade," she whispered breathlessly, overwhelmed by the elegant little gift, suddenly overcome with emotion that brought a swell of sentimental tears to her eyes. She wasn't accustomed to receiving gifts, except at Christmas and birthdays, and certainly not from Wade.

She couldn't look at him, and had to bite her lip to control herself. "It's beautiful," she repeated. "I'd like to wear it tonight." The words had barely passed her lips before she found the box removed from her fingers. Wade carefully lifted out the frail-looking necklace, and with large, surprisingly deft fingers, opened the tiny clasp. Joanna shivered as the fine chain was draped around her neck. As if he'd done so hundreds of times, Wade didn't wait for her to move her hair out of the way, but simply tunneled beneath the silken curls and fastened the clasp. The blossoming bud slid into place, but Wade's fingers lingered a moment more as a deep current of sensuality enveloped them both.

"I didn't expect this, Wade," she said with soft candor. "Thank you."

"You're welcome," he replied as his hands fell away, and an odd kind of grief began to drag her back to earth. "Are you 'bout ready to go?"

"All but my shoes." She took her bag and turned to step around him. He moved aside, then followed her into the bedroom where she slipped her feet into wheat-colored pumps that matched the handbag, and picked up a lacy shawl for later.

"You forgot something," Wade called after her just as she was about to go out the door. She turned toward him. "You're buttoned up wrong," he said, a slow smile tugging one corner of his mouth upward, giving him an impossibly rakish look.

To her utter amazement, he reached up and began to unfasten the topmost buttons of her neckline. Her knees very nearly buckled as he worked his way down to the small gap, the warmth of his fingers burning through her clothing to the sensitive swell of her breasts.

His blue eyes came up to meet hers for several electrifying moments, the primitive message she read in their depths shaking her to the core of her femininity. She couldn't move, she could barely breathe, suddenly wanting Wade more than she wanted to live.

"Don't tell me she needs help getting dressed."

Joanna jumped at Megan's sharp tone and started to pull back, but Wade didn't release the front of her dress until he'd pressed the last tiny button through its loop.

"Isn't Jake here yet?" Wade asked his sister coolly. Joanna began to think that she had imagined the past few moments with him. He had withdrawn from her, but when she made to step into the hall, his fingers closed around her elbow.

"Jake's not coming here for me. I thought you knew I would be riding with you," Megan said with a defensive toss of her head.

"Is something wrong with that little blue sports car you're so fond of?" Wade asked as he tugged gently on Joanna's elbow and started down the hall.

"It sounds a little like you don't want me to go with you, big brother," Megan said, pouting as she walked along with them.

"That all depends on whether you can behave yourself or not," he said as they started down the staircase. "You and I have an agreement, remember?"

"How can I forget?" she huffed.

"You'd better not forget," he warned gently, but said no more as he escorted them both out to his car.

"RIGHT PROUD to meet you, Mizzus Hollister." Deke Cliburn gripped Joanna's slim hand and gave it a few enthusiastic pumps.

"Joanna," she corrected softly as the balding giant beamed down at her. The hand that enveloped hers was the size of a ham.

"Purdy little thing, Wade. 'Minds me of Ina here," Deke went on in his big, full-throated baritone as he released Joanna and hooked an arm around the petite woman at his side.

"Always was a sweet-talkin' fool," Ina chortled fondly, her gray eyes twinkling up at her husband. "But I never saw the day I was half as pretty as this little girl," she exclaimed. "Glad to meet you, Joanna." Joanna shook hands with the smaller woman. The tension that had pulled her nerves unbearably tight on the long ride over began to ease its hold at the Cliburns' hearty welcome.

"I'm glad to meet you, too," she murmured with a nod as she clutched her handbag and nervously adjusted the shawl she'd folded and draped over her arm. She and Wade stood for several minutes with Megan and the Cliburns as more guests arrived and gravitated toward their small group, where they were promptly welcomed, then introduced to Joanna. Before long her head was buzzing with a confusion of names and faces. She was certain that at least a hundred guests had arrived already, with clusters more coming through the stone arch to the large back patio. She was relieved when she and Wade and Megan stepped away to a smaller, quieter group.

The savory aroma of barbecued beef filled the air as a whole steer rotated on a spit over a large pit of mesquite wood at the far end of the yard. "We barbecue the old-fashioned way here," Deke Cliburn had boomed earlier. Long tables had been set up and scattered throughout the yard, the three nearest the house currently being loaded with everything from hors d'oeuvres to dessert. A bar had been set up nearby, where four bartenders were busy.

"Oh, look, Wade," Megan said as she stepped close enough to cut Joanna out and link her arm with Wade's, "there's Lorna now, and…Jake…." Megan's voice wavered in puzzled surprise at the sight of Jake's arrival with Lorna, but she recovered herself instantly.

Joanna watched as Wade automatically turned his head to look, unable to help the spasm of jealousy she felt as Wade's gaze caught Lorna's and they exchanged a smile. She was unaware that she'd lifted her hand to her throat until her fingers touched a small budding rose.

Those rare, sweet, sensual moments they'd shared before they left for the Cliburns' were now well and truly ended. Lorna's presence had surely banished them from Wade's thoughts, while Joanna was left with a dull, aching emptiness.

She stood with brittle poise at the edge of the small

group as Jake and Lorna made their way over, a stiff smile forced on her lips.

"What would you like to drink, Joanna?" Wade asked as he leaned solicitously toward her once the initial burst of conversation was over. In spite of Megan's subtle maneuvering to edge Joanna out of the growing circle of friends, Wade had tactfully separated himself from his sister and kept Joanna by his side. He'd also managed to control any outward sign of his attraction to Lorna after those first few moments, and for that, Joanna was grateful.

"A soft drink, if they have any," she responded quietly, and Wade walked off in the direction of the bar with Jake, who was getting drinks for both Megan and Lorna.

Megan immediately dominated Lorna's attention until everyone had drinks and a few more couples wandered over to their group. From then until they ate, Joanna contributed little to the conversation that floated animatedly around her, careful not to let her mild feeling of depression show as she appeared to be absorbed in what was being said.

Once or twice she caught Jake staring at her and she smiled, but she felt like little more than a shadow at her husband's elbow until Wade's big hand came around her and rested in loose possession at her waist. It was a gesture that kindled a warm, bittersweet kind of happiness in her, and she had to work hard to remind herself it was merely for show.

Megan seemed not to have guessed that, though. Joanna frequently caught the other woman's eyes on her, blazing green with anger when alighting on Joanna, then turning merry and sweet when directed toward anyone else.

When a casual flex of Wade's arm brought Joanna close against his side, she slipped her hand daringly around his waist. She was, after all, Mrs. Wade Hollister. If her action upset Wade's spoiled sister, Joanna couldn't quite find it in her heart to feel too sympathetic.

At last the beef was served up in succulent slices. The delicious meal also included everything from pickles and relishes, to crisp salads and baked potatoes and corn to an assortment of fresh fruits and fancy desserts. Everyone helped themselves generously from the food-laden tables. After dinner a small country-and-western band began playing softly.

"Would you like to dance, Joanna?" Wade asked her as more and more couples strolled onto the dance floor.

The very thought of being in Wade's arms for minutes at a time sent a ripple of excitement through her, but Joanna was forced to shake her head, wishing with all her heart that she didn't have to refuse.

"Probably can't dance, either," Megan said with a snicker, though softly enough that only Wade and Joanna heard her.

Wade got to his feet then, and Joanna didn't look up, figuring he would step over to Lorna and ask her to dance now that he'd fulfilled whatever obligation he'd felt to ask his wife to dance first. It was just as well, she told herself. She'd rather be a wallflower because she'd never learned to dance than be one because her husband preferred to dance with the woman he loved.

"Joanna?" Wade was holding out his hand to her and she glanced up from his hard, opened palm into the compelling shadows and well-formed contours of his face.

"Megan is right," she admitted softly before her gaze skittered away, certain that was the end of it. Instead, she felt her hand lifted off her lap and enfolded in the callused warmth of Wade's as he drew her to her feet.

"Then it's time you learned," he said, leading her to the dance floor. Joanna moved stiltedly at his side, her face going pale as she realized she would be learning to dance in front of a large audience. Her breath seemed to have caught on a huge gulp of air. She almost succeeded in tugging her hand from Wade's as they reached the floor and she began to panic.

"N-not in front of all these…people," she whispered to him, her eyes darting to the dancers on the floor, as well as those who sat or stood in the area talking and watching.

Ignoring her plea, Wade gathered her into his arms and she went rigid with embarrassment. "Relax, Joanna," he murmured, holding her slightly away from him. "It's an easy dance. Move your feet like this." Wade demonstrated the simple step long enough for Joanna to catch on before he pulled her closer. "But you've got to relax." The big hand on the back of her waist pressed until she was fitted snugly against him. "That's the way," he whispered, his eyes burning down into hers as a delicious languor began to seep into her blood.

Wade moved confidently, unself-consciously, the male heat of his body radiating through the soft cotton barrier of her dress. The muscled shoulder beneath her hand felt like iron, the well-defined construction inviting her fingers to explore. It was all she could do to resist the urge. When the music ended, Joanna began to pull away.

"Not yet," Wade cautioned as his arm contracted to keep her close. "You and I are just getting started."

Joanna stared up into his eyes, seeing that the vivid blue was nearly engulfed by his widening pupils, knowing she'd heard quite clearly another meaning in his choice of words, yet fearing she hadn't. She forgot about the crowd of guests, letting him sweep her around the dance floor at will, amazed at how easily she followed his lead. After a few dances she began to feel comfortable with the different steps. At last Wade led her off the dance floor for something to drink.

"Let me get it, Wade," Megan offered cheerfully when they returned to where she and some of her friends were sitting. "Clem and Sharon haven't met Joanna yet," she explained as she flitted away from the group and headed toward the refreshment table for some punch.

Wade made the introductions while Megan was

gone, all the while keeping his arm around Joanna's waist. Jake and Lorna were nowhere in sight, and several furtive glances at Wade told her that he wasn't constantly looking for Lorna, either. Joanna tried to suppress the thrill of hope stirring inside her; she had to remember that Wade wasn't likely to be making calf eyes at Lorna in public.

"Here you are, Joanna," Megan said as she stepped up and handed Joanna the first glass of punch. "You look so hot and tired," she sympathized in an overly sweet drawl before she handed Wade his glass.

The punch was icy cold as it hit her throat, slaking her thirst with an odd kind of bite that she paid little attention to after the first burning sting. The slushy, fruity taste was so appealing that she didn't mind the slightly bitter tang that mingled subtly with it.

The next hour passed rapidly as they walked through the crowd and mingled with the other guests until Joanna felt less shy of the great number of people. Wade knew everyone and everyone seemed to like him. She was surprised that the friendship and admiration they felt for Wade was automatically extended to her without reservation.

Wade's eyes touched Joanna's frequently, and neither he nor she made a move that the other didn't see. He actually seemed to enjoy being with her as much as she enjoyed being with him, she realized with some amazement. Somehow, knowing that served to heighten her growing excitement and encourage the romantic tenderness that had begun to weave its way between them.

A little while later, Joanna saw Jake and Lorna together, noticing with secret dismay that Wade had,
too.

"Why don't you ask Lorna to dance?" she said to
him. She sipped from her third glass of punch and
felt her good mood begin to plummet.

"Why?" he asked, his eyes probing the softness of
hers.

Joanna shrugged. "I'd certainly understand it if
you'd like to dance with Lorna, or spend some time
with her. You've given me such a good time tonight
that I'd like you to have a good time, too."

"What makes you think I haven't been having a
good time?" Joanna's eyes wavered from the quick
flare of temper in his. "Finish your punch," he grumbled. When she'd drunk a little more than half and
had started to set it on a nearby table, he took it from
her and finished it for her, frowning at the empty glass
after he did.

Joanna's head spun a bit as Wade walked her to
the dance floor and pulled her into his arms. "You
underestimate yourself, Joanna," he said in a low,
rough drawl as he whirled her around to the music,
sending her senses reeling. She was grateful when the
band slowed to a ballad and Wade settled her small,
soft body against the lean length of his own.

She gazed up at him helplessly, powerless against
his touch, his attention, and the slow seduction of
being with him. Tonight was like a fairy tale, and she
could no more resist loving him than she could deny
herself breath. Alarmed and saddened by the knowl-

edge that she'd fallen in love with him, she lowered her eyes to his shirtfront and melted a little closer, instinctively wanting to hoard every moment they had left of their marriage.

Each move he made seemed more sensuous than the last, and she couldn't help the fine threads of tension that began to pull taut within her, or the way her fingers finally gave in to the urge to trace the definition of bone and sinew beneath her hand.

Wade's arm tightened then, holding her so close she could feel the hardness of his body imprinting itself on hers. Though she was inexperienced, even she knew the state of his arousal, and a deep flush crept into her cheeks.

He can't be responding to me, she told herself as she cast a careful glance around for Lorna. As if to reclaim her full attention, Wade bent down, his warm breath filtering through her hair as he rested his smooth jaw against her temple. Joanna closed her eyes, letting her nostrils fill with the clean leather and after-shave scent of him as her pulse began to beat swift and light and with faint irregularity.

Wade slid his cheek downward, nuzzling aside her hair to burrow close to her ear. Without thinking, Joanna turned her head slightly and pressed her soft mouth against the satiny warmth of his neck, unable to keep her lips from lingering for another taste of the smooth texture she hadn't expected. She felt the sudden tremor that shook Wade's big body, and went breathless as his arm tightened in reaction. And then his tongue tip found the shell of her ear in tender retaliation.

Joanna didn't remember where they were after that moment, swamped by the thick warmth that cascaded over her and turned her bones to liquid. The feel of Wade's body and the sharp needles of pleasure his mouth bestowed were the only reality. They'd even stopped pretending to dance as they swayed to a stop at the edge of the dance floor, and Joanna's hands found their way around his neck.

Wade's lips traveled from her ear to the delicate line of her cheekbone before he lowered them to find her mouth. Slowly, deliberately, he nibbled at her, coaxing her lips to open hungrily to his.

Wildly, with an abandon that would have shocked her normally, Joanna feasted on Wade's mouth, meeting the texture of his searching tongue with tiny bold strokes of her own, until Wade moaned and slowly ended the kiss.

"I think we'd better go home and finish this right," he rasped. Joanna felt as if she were drowning as she opened glazed eyes to the burning blue of his, and realized what he was saying. She could only nod as Wade turned to lead her from the dance floor.

Her legs were unsteady as she walked at Wade's side, grateful when they reached the spot where she'd left her handbag and shawl, so that she had a moment to gather her strength. Wade draped her shawl around her shoulders and wrapped his arm around her waist as they thanked the Cliburns for their hospitality, then headed for Wade's car. Neither of them gave a thought to Megan or how she would get back to the Ten Star.

The long ride home was silent after Wade drew her over next to him and pulled onto the empty highway. Joanna snuggled against his shoulder, finding the hard muscles surprisingly comfortable as she fought the strange sleepiness that weighted her eyelids and suspended every thought from her mind—except the knowledge that Wade couldn't wait to get her home.

Would they make love? she wondered dazedly, not realizing until Wade groaned that her small hand was absently stroking his hard thigh.

"Don't stop," he said as she started to pull away. From then on, Joanna glanced occasionally at his stern profile, glorying in her newfound ability to arouse him as she watched the sternness soften to a look of intense pleasure. When they reached the Ten Star and Wade pulled up in front of the big house and switched off the engine, Joanna was bold enough to reach up and turn his face toward hers for a deep searing kiss that left them both breathless.

"I'm not sure what's happening to us, Joanna, but I like it," he whispered huskily once they reached the front door and he had kissed her again. Joanna was unable to form a coherent word, afraid to give voice to what she was feeling. After opening the door, Wade turned and swept her up in his arms, carrying her through the softly lit entry hall and up the carpeted stairs.

Joanna felt a spiraling excitement as he passed her bedroom door without hesitation and walked into his own room with her. He set her gently on his bed, then pulled the comforter and top sheet down before he stepped away and closed the door. Joanna heard the click as he turned the lock, feeling the fine tension in her lower parts pull taut with the knowledge that Wade wanted her in total privacy.

CHAPTER EIGHT

"LET'S HAVE SOME LIGHT," Wade rasped. A match tip flared, and a small flame sputtered softly to life in the antique kerosene lamp that sat on a nearby chest. Joanna watched while he adjusted the wick, until the darkness in the big room brightened to a dim golden glow.

In scant moments he removed his boots, using the iron bootjack at the foot of the bed, then started toward her. She couldn't look away from the predatory spark in the glittering blue gaze that moved slowly over her. Wade removed his vest and tossed it onto a nearby chair. She stared, wide-eyed, as he reached for the buttons of his shirt; her heart pounding, she followed his hands as they moved leisurely downward. The silver belt buckle glittered dully in the soft light, as he tugged his shirt from the waistband of his slacks and peeled it off.

Still Joanna couldn't take her eyes from him, fascinated by the play of muscle and sinew in his wide shoulders and powerful body, feeling herself melt as her gaze wandered over his hair-matted chest to his flat, lightly furred stomach.

Wade stepped closer, stopping just inches in front

of her. His eyes darkened to midnight blue as he crouched and reached for her ankle. Unhurriedly he pulled off both her shoes, his big hands stroking warmly upward, as if memorizing the feel of her. Long, firm fingers pushed the hem of her skirt higher. She shivered, her eyes half closing; warmth slowly spread over her body, and she felt all her tension ebb away.

Wade straightened, and the mattress gave with his weight as he sat beside her and turned her gently toward him. Callused fingertips skimmed lightly over the hollow beneath her cheekbone, then threaded tenderly into her hair as he leaned closer.

The touch of his lips stopped her breath. She slid her hands up his rough chest to wrap her arms around his neck, unable to help the sudden flash fire of passion that blazed through her as her mouth opened and clung hungrily to his.

"Not so fast, Joanna," he whispered, tearing his mouth from hers and nuzzling the sensitive shell of her ear. His embrace changed suddenly and she felt keen disappointment until she realized he was merely lifting her to place her in the middle of the turned-down bed.

His big body covered hers as he lay down, his teeth nipping her earlobe and sending tiny shivers of delight coursing through her veins. She hugged him close, her slim fingers ranging eagerly over his solid flesh.

She was a woman who had never expected to be desired by a man, least of all Wade. His responses to her that evening had infused her with a kind of sensual confidence she'd once believed alien to her nature. But she was in love with him, and the instinctive need to consummate that love was becoming a compelling force that dominated her every action. She felt no warning, no sense of caution, as she gave herself wholeheartedly to the magic of his lips and hands....

Much later, Joanna slept, lying as if boneless beneath the warm solidity of Wade's body. But soon the demanding pressure of his mouth on hers brought her awake. Twice more they made love, and not once during their long night together did Joanna allow herself a thought for tomorrow.

JOANNA PULLED HER HORSE to a halt on the crest of a high sunny rise, inhaling deeply as her eyes dropped from the horizon. The wind ruffled her shirt, gently fanning the fine mist of perspiration from her skin and sending a cooling relaxation through her, as she untied her canteen and took several swallows of water.

She'd been out since just after sunrise, riding over miles of land, sorting through the confusion of thoughts and feelings that had haunted her since those last moments with Wade as she'd watched him sleep and finally regained her sanity.

The shock of what she'd done, and the wanton abandon with which she'd done it, still jarred her. She didn't feel like herself anymore, and couldn't help but be a little frightened of the intensely passionate nature Wade's lovemaking had brought to life in her.

She'd had a strong taste of what loving Wade could

be like, and her mind was constantly filled with erotic images of the two of them together. Her fear of rejection had always restricted her ability to give even slight affection to anyone before, but last night she had felt no fear when she gave herself so totally to Wade. There had been no thought, just a heated mixture of emotion and desire that had leapt up and consumed them both. She still didn't understand how it had happened.

And now the floodgates of her heart had burst open, leaving her fully exposed and vulnerable to Wade.

Tears rushed into her eyes, but Joanna stubbornly forced them back. Tears had got her precious little in life. They hadn't brought back her mother from the grave, hadn't got her a better childhood with her aunt, nor persuaded her father to let her grow up on the Double L. Giving way to them had only made her caretakers more impatient with her.

That was why she'd left Wade's bed early and slipped onto the balcony to retreat to her room. It wasn't hard to guess that the next time he woke up, it would be daylight, and he'd regret making love to her when it was Lorna he truly wanted. She didn't think she could have remained dry-eyed had she been forced to listen to him tell her so.

But she felt stronger now. It was just after noon, and she'd had hours to get used to the idea that it was easy for some men to avail themselves of the nearest willing woman when they couldn't have the one they craved. Though the room last night had been lit, the light had been very dim. Joanna's hair was not as bright as Lorna's, but close enough in the shadows for Wade to be able to make believe that the woman he was making love to so thoroughly was Lorna instead of her.

Jealousy and anguish tore through her, but Joanna forced her attention to the range around her. The long, slow pulse of wind rippling through the grasses, the buzz of bees gathering nectar and the occasional birdsong touched her aching soul like a symphony of consolation.

She'd seen several pronghorn antelope in the hours she'd been riding, and quite early that morning she'd seen what looked like either a coyote or gray fox hurrying to its den after a night of hunting. She'd come across dozens of black-tailed jackrabbits, their black-tipped ears standing like twin sentinels—until she rode too close and they streaked off into the grass.

She was learning quickly which parts of the Ten Star had more rattlesnakes than others, though the snakes could be found almost anywhere. It was some comfort to know that they could feel the vibration of her horse's hooves and usually slithered well out of the way before she even spotted them.

The bluebonnets were in bloom, in some places looking like a pool of blue flowers. A bit of wild verbena grew here and there, along with the pale lavender of heart's delight and the more exotic purple paintbrush.

She turned her head at the intrusion of an odd clacking sound. Nudging her horse in the direction of the sound, she soon spotted a solitary little roadrunner. Long-legged, long-tailed, the bird stood on a small rock while it tried to gulp down a tiny lizard. She watched until her horse snorted and the bird scurried off.

Joanna sat back in the saddle, pulling off her Stetson to lift her face toward the sun. Life was throbbing all around her, and she realized suddenly that she was a living, breathing part of it. A deep peace settled in her troubled soul as she sensed she had found her place.

She belonged here as she had nowhere else. The nearby Double L was hers, and she'd never have to leave, never have to give up this new life or the new person she was becoming. She felt more a part of nature's cycle here where living was simple, yet a challenge; she felt more attuned to nature, and now, more in touch with herself.

A soft, sweetly sad smile came to her lips. If last night was the only night of loving she'd ever know with Wade, she'd try to be satisfied.

JOANNA STEPPED into the kitchen and silently hung her hat on its customary peg before she started toward the back stairs. She hurried up the staircase, not waiting for anyone to acknowledge that she'd returned, but assuming that someone had heard her come in. Consuelo was never too far from the kitchen around supper time, and she somehow always kept track of everyone's comings and goings, whether it was mealtime or not.

Joanna had just reached her room, when she recognized the purposeful thud of boots on the front stairs. She closed the door gently behind her, wishing it wasn't Wade who was coming up—not yet.

Although she'd mentally rehearsed what she would say to him a dozen different ways that day, she wasn't certain she could go through with it. She'd never done anything quite like what she was planning, nor had she wanted to, and there was a good chance Wade would beat her to it.

Joanna felt panicked. She couldn't reject Wade, but then again, she couldn't bear to have him reject her. Of course, she wouldn't actually be rejecting him, she reminded herself; what she had planned was more a denial of the importance of the night before.

A few seconds later he knocked at the door. She waited for as long as she dared before she called out for him to come in. As he stepped inside she edged closer to the balcony doors, unable to meet his gaze. Her sunburned cheeks flushed as she turned away from him until her face was almost in profile.

"I had men out looking for you for hours."

Wade's low voice moved over her like rough velvet, and she had to fight the images and sensations it provoked as he walked closer. She felt nearly smothered by the impact of his maleness when he finally stopped, and only two feet separated them.

"I know," she murmured. "Lester—isn't that his name?—told me. I'm sorry you went to all that trouble."

"Why didn't you come back with him?" Wade asked.

She turned even farther away from him, pretending to stare out the glass doors onto the patio below. "I needed to be by myself for a while," she answered. "And," she added, her face flushing a bit darker as she forced herself to go on, "I was embarrassed about the way I...behaved last night."

There was complete silence from Wade, but Joanna couldn't look at him to discern why. She was truly embarrassed about the night before, especially when she recalled how uninhibited she'd been, how man-hungry she must have seemed to him. She still cringed inside when she thought of the things she'd said and done with him.

She raised a hand to rub her fingertips nervously over her forehead. "I—I don't know why I was like that, but I can assure you it will never happen again," she vowed softly. Her slim shoulders straightened as she dropped her hand, and her chin came up a fraction.

Wade said nothing for the longest time, but finally spoke. "I'm afraid Megan had something to do with last night," he began, earning himself Joanna's startled attention for a moment before her eyes veered ashamedly away.

"How?" she ventured unsteadily, unable to imagine how Megan could possibly have had any part in what she and Wade had done.

Wade ran an agitated hand through his dark hair. "She made sure you got some spiked punch. As I reckon it, she was hoping you'd have too much to drink and embarrass yourself."

Joanna took a deep, weary breath, then shook her head. Megan had certainly succeeded.

"I apologize, Joanna," Wade said grimly. "Megan will be offering her own apology later."

Joanna sensed Wade's discomfort, and chanced a quick glance at his face, relieved that his eyes were downcast for that brief moment. She caught the subtle change in his expression and glanced away, tensing herself for what was coming.

After a few more strained seconds, Wade began, "About last night—"

"I'd rather not talk about it," Joanna cut in swiftly, as the tiny muscles in her throat contracted. "We both know it was a colossal mistake. I'm not even in love with you," she managed.

The room went deadly quiet. "That's not what you said last night," he reminded her callously.

Joanna felt her balance teeter as she sought desperately to collect her thoughts and offer a believable excuse. "I don't think I can be held fully accountable for last night," she said primly. "As you pointed out, Megan made certain I was drinking spiked punch." Joanna's lips formed an unhappy line as she strained to remember her words.

"And that was my first time like that with a man," she admitted, her voice wavering ever so slightly as her control faltered and embarrassment threatened to overwhelm her. "You were very…experienced. I might have said anything."

Joanna made a small dismissive gesture as she fought for just the right touch of icy disdain in her soft voice. "Just because we had sex doesn't mean there's any love between us, or that I want to stay married to you. In fact—" she shoved her hands into her jeans pockets to hide their tremors as she babbled on a little wildly "—I want to speed up our divorce. Last night made things a bit more complicated than either of us wants." Joanna paused, swallowing away the huge lump that seemed to grow larger with every word, deeply unnerved by Wade's ongoing silence. "And frankly, I'm quite uncomfortable with you now."

"We...didn't use any protection," he reminded her unexpectedly and her eyes flew to his, unable to conceal her alarm. "Is there even a chance you might be pregnant?"

Joanna's sunburned face paled. "N-no. There's no...chance," she lied unsteadily.

There was a small chance, since her cycle was sometimes irregular, but she wouldn't be able to bear it if Wade either suggested or insisted upon an abortion because he had no use for a child by her. The very thought of abortion had always repulsed her, but never more than now when she herself might be carrying a tiny, newly conceived life within her womb. The child might not be the product of a mutually loving relationship, but she loved Wade and she knew she would love his child.

"Are you sure?" he persisted, his eyes narrowing as if he'd read her mind.

"Yes," she said firmly, hearing the certainty in her voice and drawing from it. "But just so you'll know,'' she added with a touch of defiance, ''it would be my child. I wouldn't destroy it just because I was too drunk and too foolish to keep myself out of your bed. Or because its existence might create some embarrassment for you and Megan.''

Wade's expression went black. ''I wouldn't allow you to destroy it. But just so *you'll* know,'' he growled, taking a menacing step toward her, ''the child would be mine, too, and my first heir. It would stay on the Ten Star.''

Joanna stared at Wade, her face frozen in shock at his vehemence before she could recover herself. It had never occurred to her that he would want a child by her. Hearing his declaration jolted her.

''There is no child,'' she insisted fearfully, suddenly terrified that if there were, Wade would find some way to keep her baby and drive her away. The mere thought brought tears welling into her eyes. Badly shaken, she turned away to hide her crumpling expression.

Wade cursed softly and took that last step toward her. ''That was a little rough, Joanna,'' he rasped as he gripped her arm and turned her to face him. ''I didn't mean....''

The same shock wave of desire that had rocked her at his touch had struck him—she could see it in the way his eyes went dark when her startled gaze sped up to his. Suddenly he released her as if she'd burned him, his face turning to granite, his blue gaze firing with what she thought was silent rage.

''How soon will you know whether you're pregnant or not?'' he demanded, the tenderness she'd heard in his voice just a moment ago vanished.

"I just told you—"

"I heard what you just told me," he snarled as he leaned down and his face came close to hers. "But you'll never be a very good liar."

Joanna somehow managed to maintain contact with the laser intensity of his gaze, but it was like staring into a blast furnace. Her small chin lifted to a stubborn angle.

"Even if I were pregnant," she emphasized the *if*, "how soon I'll know or won't know is no concern of yours."

"We'll see, Joanna," he growled, the warning in his low voice sending chills down her spine. "We'll see." And with that he stormed out of her room, yanking the door closed with enough force to rattle the balcony doors.

Later, after an uneasy supper with Wade and Megan, Joanna made her excuses and slipped upstairs to bed. But tired as she was after losing so much sleep the night before, she didn't rest well.

What would happen if she was carrying Wade's child? she fretted silently, truly frightened. But to her great surprise, she was infinitely more frightened at the thought that the miracle might *not* have happened.

"MORNIN', JOANNA."

Jake Terrell grinned down at her as he thumbed back his Stetson.

"Good morning, Jake," she said with a smile. She

finished tightening the cinch on her saddle, and let the stirrup down. "Wade's on the phone up at the house," she told Jake, assuming he'd come down to the barn expecting to see Wade about something. "Unless you were looking for Megan."

Jake's grinning countenance darkened slightly. "I sure ain't looking for Megan," he said with a chuckle, and Joanna laughed softly.

"That's probably wise," she agreed, but didn't elaborate. To say that Megan was a bit on the sour side that morning would have been putting it mildly. The apology that Wade had required of Megan apparently wasn't setting well, even though she had yet to make it or even to hint that she owed Joanna one. Which was fine with Joanna, for she knew full well that any apology Megan might make to her would be insincere and probably downright condescending.

"Came over looking for you," Jake said.

Joanna welcomed the warmth in his gaze after her tense breakfast at the Hollister table, and couldn't help returning his smile, her spirits improving at Jake's sunny disposition.

Jake continued, "Consuelo said you'd be down at the barn. I wanted to see if you'd give me a rain check on that dance I didn't collect at the Cliburns' night before last."

Joanna's smile stiffened a bit at the mention of the dance, her mind automatically replaying what had happened later and ending on the thought of how little that night of lovemaking had meant to Wade. And now she had to pretend it meant little to her, too. Already the effort was beginning to cost her.

Not two days had passed, yet time was dragging along so slowly for her that she felt she'd lived years since then. She wasn't certain she could carry on the cold, unfeeling little charade she'd had to perform that morning at breakfast. Only she was aware of just how deep and traumatic a denial of her love it had been when she repressed her still-tender emotions in order to ignore Wade casually as if he didn't exist, or to turn a shallow, indifferent gaze on him whenever he spoke to her.

"Joanna?" Jake's mellow drawl drew her out of her thoughts, and she realized he was still waiting for her to say something.

"Of course," she answered swiftly. "A rain check would be fine with me."

Jake's dark brows came together as his lips curved in amusement. Joanna had the sudden uncomfortable feeling that she'd missed something he'd said. But Jake merely grinned as he looked away and reached out to run a big hand over Lucky's sleek red neck.

"Things must be better between you and Wade," he commented then, taking Joanna totally by surprise as he patted Lucky. He missed the raw pain that came into her eyes before she could lower her lashes and look away to hide it. "And if that's what you want, I'm glad for you, honey," was all he said, but he conveyed the idea that he thought there was a more than even chance she and Wade would stay together.

When Joanna was able to meet Jake's soft brown

gaze, she managed a facsimile of a smile and quickly changed the subject. "When is roundup on the Little Mesquite?" she asked, knowing that the next two weeks on the Ten Star were going to be devoted to roundup preparations. And by the time roundup was finished on the Ten Star, the Double L would be a week or so into its roundup.

"We've got another month yet," Jake said. "This is your first roundup, isn't it?"

Joanna nodded, a genuine smile on her lips. She welcomed the distraction of talking about something she looked forward to. "I can't wait. Of course," she added wryly, "I doubt anyone will think I'm much help, but I intend to try."

Jake chuckled at her enthusiasm. "You'll do just fine."

"I hope so," she said, her expression sobering a bit. "It's very important to me."

"No one expects you to ride out there and handle yourself like you've been working with horses and cattle for most of your life," he counseled gently.

"I know, but I want to do well." The earnestness in her eyes conveyed just how important it was to her.

"You will," he said, his drawl gravelly as he lifted his hand to brush his knuckles down her cheek. "You will."

"Hello, Jake."

Joanna started slightly, and Jake dropped his hand as they both turned their heads to look at Megan.

"Joanna," Megan added politely, her green eyes

snapping a warning before they swung back to rest on Jake. "You should have stayed up at the house, Jake. There's still plenty of hot coffee, and a big piece of that cinnamon coffee cake Consuelo whipped up for breakfast."

"Didn't come for cake and coffee, Meg," Jake said, his mouth set in a half grin that wasn't echoed by the look in his eyes. Joanna wasn't comfortable standing in the subtle crosscurrent of tension that arced between Jake and Megan. She was about to reach for Lucky's reins and leave, when Wade walked into the barn.

"Morning, Jake."

The tension Joanna had felt between Jake and Megan was mild compared to the sudden charge of hostility between Jake and Wade. Both men stood facing each other, the few feet separating them fairly crackling with animosity.

Wade's stance, with his feet braced slightly apart, was rigid, every muscle seeming to stand out in aggressive relief against the flimsy barrier of denim and chambray. Jake was as lithe and limber as well-worked leather. It was only in the flex of his jaw muscles and the hard challenging gleam in his dark eyes that he seemed a match for Wade's virile toughness.

All at once Joanna recognized what was going on between the two men. Jake had taken Lorna to the Cliburns' barbecue, and Wade was clearly jealous. This little display of feather ruffling was somehow more acceptable now than it would have been at the barbecue.

Agony gripped her heart, twisting it viciously, and it was all she could do to retain her composure and not grab Lucky's reins and flee. If she'd suffered any delusions, however feeble, about a future with Wade, they were now well and truly dashed. Wade's future was with Lorna.

"You wouldn't be planning to fly into San Antone sometime this week, would you?" Megan asked Jake, successfully breaking the tension between the two men as she sidled up to Jake and touched his arm. But Jake didn't pull his intent gaze from Wade's until Megan tugged on his shirt sleeve.

"Might be," Jake responded noncommittally, scowling faintly until Megan managed to look genuinely hurt. Then he seemed to relent. "I'm going tomorrow."

"There are some things I'd like to pick up. Think I could go along?" Megan flashed him her most engaging smile.

A man would have to be made of iron not to be just a little persuaded by the look Megan was giving Jake, Joanna thought enviously. But beguiling men into doing her bidding was a feminine art Joanna had never learned, for she felt she possessed too little of a basic prerequisite—confidence in her ability to attract men.

That assumption was reinforced when she glanced over at Wade and suddenly seemed to catch his attention. It was as if she'd never seen him angry before. Or perhaps this was more rage than anger, she wasn't sure. She only knew that his eyes were burning into hers, his face like a great dark monolith. It was a look that frightened her, letting her see just how much he resented being chained to her and barred from official competition for his beloved Lorna.

"I'll be seein' you, Joanna," Jake said.

Joanna glanced over at him, her lips stretching into what passed for a smile. "I'll be looking forward to it," she said with gentle sincerity, and Jake's eyes gleamed for a second before he nodded to Wade and turned to leave.

Megan went along with him, and the moment they were out the door, Joanna reached for Lucky's reins.

"I'm going over to Lorna's. Want to come along?" Wade's voice was harsh, almost belligerent.

"I'd rather not," she told him quietly as she started to lead Lucky toward the barn door.

Wade smoothly removed the reins from her loose grip, and Joanna turned back to him in surprise. "I'd like you to come." Wade's voice had softened somewhat, but not his dark expression.

Joanna shook her head slightly in confusion. "Why?" she asked, then suddenly discerned the answer on her own. "So I can see how in love you are with Lorna?" she dared, lashing out at him, unable to conceal the volatile mixture of hurt and anger she felt.

"No, Joanna." His brows had lowered, some of his anger gone, but he was impatient with her all the same.

"You needn't worry," she said stiffly. "I'm not falling in love with you because of what's happened." It was amazing how easily the lie rolled off her tongue when she was fighting to preserve at least a shred of what pride she had left.

Wade's face hardened, and a blatantly skeptical look came into his eyes.

"But I'm not made of stone," she felt forced to admit. "Of course I have some feeling toward you. Doesn't every woman feel that way about the first man?" Joanna was shaking inside. "However, I can assure you it's nothing you need to worry about."

She reached for the reins, but Wade's grip held them fast.

"I don't want to go, Wade," she repeated. Didn't he understand how awkward it would be for her to see Lorna now? Under the circumstances, Joanna felt like the other woman in a cheap fling. "I *won't* go," she insisted then. Her quick tug on the reins gained their release.

"Suit yourself." With that, he turned and walked away from her, leaving her at the mercy of a jealous imagination.

CHAPTER NINE

"HAVE YOU LOST something, *señora*?"

Joanna jerked guiltily, turning her head to see Consuelo standing in the open doorway. The puzzled frown on the Mexican woman's face gave way to a look of dawning perception as Joanna straightened from frantically running her fingers through the thick carpet beside Wade's bed.

Joanna had waited until she was certain Wade and Megan were both gone and Consuelo was busy before she came upstairs to search for the small rose necklace Wade had given her. She'd looked everywhere else for it in the past few days, finally concluding that the last time she could clearly recall having it around her neck she had been in this room, in Wade's bed.

The only alternative was that it had slipped from her neck in the shower that next morning and had been washed down the drain. If that was so, then it was lost forever. Joanna couldn't bear the thought.

Her mind had been in such a turmoil the morning after the barbecue that she hadn't thought of the necklace. Not used to wearing much jewelry, she hadn't missed it until she'd fled from the house and gone riding all day. By then, she assumed it was in her room somewhere, although she didn't actually recall taking it off. Later, when all her efforts to find it turned up nothing, she'd begun to worry. Checking Wade's room now was a last resort.

"Was it perhaps a gold rose on a chain, *señora*?" Consuelo asked, the knowing glimmer that came into her dark eyes subduing Joanna's relief.

Joanna had not intended anyone to know she'd ever been in Wade's room, but now, glancing nervously toward the bed, she realized that Consuelo would have to know she'd been here before.

"Yes, it was," she said as she got to her feet, her cheeks bright with color.

"I saw it in the small tray on the *señor*'s bureau," Consuelo said, gesturing.

Joanna hurried across the room, but her heart sank when she saw that the polished wooden tray was empty.

"Perhaps he has put it away somewhere, *señora*. Shall I—"

"No, Consuelo. No, don't bother." Joanna's lips tightened into a self-conscious smile. "Thank you anyway."

"As you wish, *señora*." She nodded, her expression not showing the disapproval Joanna expected. "Is there anything I may do for you?"

"Oh, no," Joanna said quickly. She was still not accustomed to having things done for her, such as the cooking, laundry and cleaning that the housekeeper had taken care of for her these past weeks. Knowing how busy Consuelo was running the Hollister household made her refrain from causing the woman any more work than she already took upon herself. Joanna automatically declined every offer Consuelo made to wait on her further. ''Thank you, anyway,'' she added as Consuelo nodded, then turned and left her alone.

Joanna didn't leave right away, but paused to glance once more around the large, comfortably furnished room. Like every other room in the house, it contained rich wooden furniture, many pieces of which were antiques, their surfaces polished to a deep, dark luster. The thick plush of a brown area rug covered most of the wooden floor, but the rest of the room was decorated in varied shades of blue, mostly dark but with lighter accents. Being there again did odd things to her, and she felt a strong contraction of desire as her thoughts melted into her memory of that night.

But it would not happen again. Wade was so remote now, polite but almost unapproachable. Every uncomfortable moment she spent with him, coupled with the many hours he avoided her, merely underscored the degree of emotional estrangement she was forced to endure.

To share something with Wade as intimate as a night of lovemaking, then to be subjected to his relentless indifference, was almost more than she could stand. But she did stand it, appearing as aloof and removed from him as he was from her. It had slowly become a test of her endurance.

Until she had been unable to find the necklace. The little gold trinket was more precious to her than she'd first realized. Certainly she was a fool to read too much into the gift, but she couldn't seem to help herself. That little rose necklace might turn out to be the only physical proof she would ever have, aside from her lost virginity, that those few hours with him had happened at all. She'd already lost hope that she had become pregnant, dismissing the possibility as so much wishful thinking.

But if Consuelo had found the necklace and placed it in the tray, Wade must know she'd lost it. The fact that he hadn't returned it to her hurt deeply. Perhaps he regretted giving it to her.

Joanna heard a door closing downstairs, followed quickly by the sound of Consuelo's voice. Not wanting anyone else to catch her in Wade's room, she hurried out, slipping soundlessly down the front stairs to return to the den.

A few minutes later, she heard Wade coming down the hall, the fine threads of tension inside her drawing tight in anticipation as she listened to his approach, then twisting into an ache of despair as he strode in and spared her no more than a flicker of a glance.

"Are you about done with that?" he asked as he walked over to sift through the stack of mail on the edge of the desk.

He was referring to the Double L books. A while ago he'd left her to go over them and make certain everything was up to date. Joanna had finished the task before going upstairs to look for the necklace, and had just been glancing through them again to kill

time as she mulled over what she planned to discuss
with Wade.

"Yes," she said, closing the top ledger and rising
from the big swivel chair. She cleared her throat
softly, clenching her profile and stepped around to a
front corner of the desk.

"I made some phone calls this afternoon," she began, her voice a bit unsteady. "There are several
things I want to have done to the main house at the
Double L before I move in, so I spoke to a few contractors." Wade didn't look up, but appeared to be
listening, so she took a quick breath and went on.
"Two of them will be meeting me there early next
week to look over the house and give me some esti-
mates. I'm hoping one of them will start on the structural changes within the month."

That earned her a brief, piercing look that wavered,
then swept downward before it swung away. "That
was a good idea," he murmured as he finished sorting
and hefted a handful of junk mail toward the waste-
basket. Joanna stared at him in some surprise, but
managed to conceal it when he looked her way again.

"I made a few calls of my own this morning," he
informed her. "I've arranged for your driving lessons
to start the week after next, so you might as well go
ahead and find yourself a decorator to take over when
the remodeling's finished. That way," he added with
a wry twist of lips, "you'll have plenty of time to
fuss over samples and make up your mind."

"But roundup starts that week," she protested, not
understanding why he'd schedule her driving lessons

for such a busy time, then suggest she take even more time off to work with an interior decorator when there would be so much to do here.

"It does," he agreed, his eyes going the color of gunmetal, his stern expression turning almost harsh. "But I've decided it's not necessary for you to go along." From the hard look he was giving her, he wasn't about to change his mind.

Joanna was stunned. "Why not?" she got out.

Wade's face was unreadable. "You're good with horses, Joanna, but you haven't worked enough cattle to know what you're doing," he said. "Roundup is rough, hard work, even for men who've been doing it all their lives. It can also be dangerous work. Putting a greenhorn like you out there in the middle of all that is just asking for trouble, so I don't think it's a good idea to take you along."

Joanna stared, taking a deep, slow breath as she absorbed the shock and tried to restrain the burning fullness behind her eyes. Her emotions had been wrenched and battered for days, and now this seemed almost one blow too many.

Wade wasn't so concerned for her welfare, no matter what he said; he was simply determined to hurt and alienate her, to do whatever it took, just as long as she got the message loud and clear that he felt nothing for her and never would.

"Don't you think you've punished me enough for that night?" she asked candidly, shaking so hard inside that only conscious effort kept her tongue from catching and stuttering.

"You aren't being punished," Wade growled. But he couldn't meet her gaze, his eyes downcast, a muscle in his jaw flexing wildly.

"I made another call today," she said in a soft voice that was almost a whisper. "I was going to start divorce proceedings against you, but I found out I haven't met the six-month residency requirement yet."

"I could have told you that," he muttered sullenly.

"Then you should have," she said in a bit stronger voice. "And since I can't file for several more months, I insist *you* have it taken care of before roundup."

"Dammit, there isn't time," he snapped.

"You have the money and the contacts to overcome that small obstacle," she returned. Wade shot her a black look. "We both know a quick phone call to your lawyer will set everything in motion today."

Wade swore softly, then reluctantly grumbled his consent.

"With that taken care of, you shouldn't feel such a need to shove me away at every opportunity," she reasoned coolly, her emotions at last locked safely into place. "So there'll be no reason for me to miss roundup. The driving lessons can be postponed, and I can hire a decorator later."

"You're not going, Joanna," Wade said, the warning in his voice underscoring the vivid anger in his eyes. "And I don't want to hear another word about it."

IT WAS JUST BEFORE DAWN when they finished the hearty roundup breakfast Consuelo had prepared, then climbed into Wade's pickup for the long ride to one of the farthest points on the Ten Star to rendezvous with his men. The wranglers had driven the remuda there two days before, and when Wade, Joanna and Megan arrived and saddled their mounts, they joined the large group of men who would work most of the day to gather cattle from this section of range.

Joanna had been too excited to sleep well the night before and had only picked at the big breakfast she'd been served—until ill-tempered rumblings from Wade had induced her to force down more food. She couldn't risk raising his ire and chancing he'd make good on his threat to send her back to the house if she couldn't keep up.

That she was even going along at all was nothing short of miraculous, since he'd been so determined to leave her behind. Surprisingly Joanna had Megan to thank for getting Wade to reconsider. At first, when Megan discovered that Joanna wasn't to go, she hadn't seemed to care. It was later, after the next time Jake dropped by, that Megan had begun her relentless campaign to coax Wade into changing his mind.

It wasn't hard for Joanna to figure out that Megan was more concerned with the absurd notion of keeping Joanna and Jake apart than she was with championing Joanna's cause. But as long as she got to go along and work the roundup, Joanna didn't care what Megan's motivations were.

Joanna stayed close to Wade and Megan as they

rode out of the temporary camp, watching as the men split into widely separated groups of three and began to fan out to cover several square miles of rolling, brushy range.

"Pay attention," Wade grumbled as he took the coil of rope from his saddle. With a curt nod to Megan, he urged his gray gelding forward, taking off at a trot toward a thick stand of brush. Joanna followed the pair, just able to make out the big red-brown shapes scattered on the hill on the other side. Wade rode his gray through a break in the middle of the low growth, motioning to Joanna to ride her sorrel around one side while Megan went around the other.

It was Joanna's horse that the small bunch of cows and calves saw first, and just as they started to move for the cover of the brush, Wade's gray lunged quickly to intercept them.

Bawling an occasional protest, the cows milled for a moment, until Wade rode toward them, slapping his coil of rope against the leather chaps that encased his legs. The popping sound drove them in the direction he wanted them to go.

Joanna grinned at the easy beginning, but her expression fell when Wade scowled at her.

"We'll be at this all day if you don't learn to keep your eyes open and go after some cows." He nodded toward a bit of brush to her left.

Joanna turned her head, then flushed uncomfortably when she made out the shapes of another cow and calf in the undergrowth. Laying the reins along her horse's neck, she touched her heels to his sides and rode over to collect the cattle while Wade rode in the opposite direction and Megan slowly herded the small gather toward the corrals miles to the south and east.

By midday, Joanna was frustrated and disillusioned, certain Wade had handpicked the contrary animals she'd had the bad luck to go after so that she would become discouraged and give up. It was her opinion that Ten Star cattle had little sense and almost no inclination to cooperate. She was amazed at the amount of work it took to persuade one cow to move in the right direction, not to mention how much vigilance it took to *keep* it moving. Joanna had learned quickly to take nothing for granted.

Because Wade had rotated the task of chasing cattle out of the brush and herding the gather as he, Megan and Joanna worked their way south, Joanna had had a respite now and then from the wild, jouncing ride her mount had given her. The surefooted little cow pony was extremely capable, so much so that Joanna had often thought he could have done a better job without her on his back. However, he was also the most rough-gaited horse she'd ever ridden. After a few hours, Joanna longed to step down for a moment to ease her queasy stomach and give her aching backside a rest. But that wasn't possible. She sensed that they had already fallen far behind because of her inexperience.

As a result, they arrived at the camp for the midday meal more than an hour after everyone else. Wade wasn't in the best of moods and neither was Megan, but they made no disparaging remarks about Joanna's lack of skill or the way she'd slowed them down.

By the time Joanna got off her horse and made it to the chow line, she was too hungry to care what she ate as long as the serving was large. Eating and resting restored much of her natural vitality, so by the time Wade and Megan were ready, Joanna was eager to select another mount from the remuda and saddle up for an afternoon of more work.

"Why don't you try that pinto?" Wade suggested as he nodded toward a brown-and-white gelding nearby. Delighted with his colorful markings, Joanna had no problem catching him. She hoped for a smoother ride this time.

The cattle seemed to gather more easily in the afternoon, and the pinto Wade had helped her choose moved fluidly beneath her. Joanna felt much more confident as she and Wade methodically searched the rough, hilly terrain while Megan held and moved the gather.

It was midafternoon when Joanna came across the most contrary cow she'd seen all day. From the moment she urged her pinto down a long, narrow fold of land toward her, the cow had turned a wide, stubborn face in her direction, rolling her eyes warily as Joanna carefully approached. The young calf at the cow's side shadowed her every move, but Joanna believed it would present no problem, so she paid it little attention.

Suddenly the cow wheeled and bolted straight up the steep side of the hill, heedless of the bawling calf, which couldn't keep up. At the top, the cow made a sharp turn and ran wildly toward the north part of the section they'd already worked. Joanna's pinto tore up the sod as he raced after the cow, and Joanna gave him his head, wishing she knew how to do more with a rope than just slap it against her chaps.

On and on they ran, the cow managing to keep just enough ahead that the pinto couldn't maneuver to cut her off. Just as they got close enough for Joanna to make a mad swing at the cow's neck with her coiled rope, the cow skidded to a halt and whirled to head back the way they'd come.

Joanna was nearly unseated when her cow pony did the same, pivoting neatly to give chase.

They were almost back where they'd started from, when the cow met her calf and took another detour. This time, she ran for a short stand of mesquite, charging through the thickest part of the undergrowth. Joanna pulled back on her mount, unwilling to ride into all that, choosing instead to race around the edge and meet them on the other side.

It was when she'd urged her pinto around the trees and bounded over the top of a small incline that she saw Wade. But by then it was too late. Before she could pull back on the reins or yell a warning, her pinto dodged sideways—but not soon enough to avoid colliding with Wade's horse.

Joanna heard a scream as her horse struck his, not realizing, as she and Wade were thrown violently to the ground with their mounts, the scream she'd heard was her own.

"M-my God," she sobbed as the blackness faded a few minutes later and her swimming vision cleared. She was sprawled on her side on the ground. Wade lay unconscious just inches from her, his face drained of color, a dark bruise already swelling near his temple.

Stunned, Joanna reached for him, but cried out when the movement of her arm brought pain knifing into her left shoulder and back.

"Megan," she panted in a hoarse whisper, then, "Megan!" she finally shouted. She used her other arm to pull herself closer to Wade. She stretched out a hand to grip his wrist, her panic easing a bit as she felt the strong, steady pulse. "Megan!" she shouted again, noticing that this time Wade stirred slightly at the sound of her voice. "Oh, Wade," she sobbed, tears cascading down her face. "Please don't die."

It seemed forever before she heard the swift drum of hooves, and then Megan was vaulting off her horse, falling to her knees on the other side of Wade, her face almost as white as his. Megan's green eyes filled with tears as she checked for a pulse. Joanna watched helplessly, still stunned as Megan ran her hands over Wade's body searching for broken bones. Apparently satisfied, she glanced over at Joanna.

"This is your fault, isn't it?" she demanded. Joanna could only nod stupidly, the movement bringing sharp pain, as she felt herself wither beneath Megan's condemning stare.

"I—I'm s-sorry," Joanna stammered, reeling with fear and remorse.

Megan made a disgusted sound, then reached down to touch Wade's pale cheek before she jumped to her feet and leaped into the saddle to go for help.

"Please don't die," Joanna repeated hysterically once Megan had gone, forcing herself to her knees, clutching at Wade's arm when he moved his head and his eyelashes began to flutter. "I'm so, so sorry," she sobbed, delirious with fear and guilt. "I love you so much. Please don't die," she babbled wildly, her breath catching raggedly when those vividly blue eyes opened and fixed their bleary gaze on her face before slowly drifting closed.

"BY GOD, I WANT HER in here!" Wade raged, his thunderous voice echoing so loudly in his room that Joanna could hear distinctly from her own.

Consuelo murmured to her consolingly as she gently dabbed the tear-streaked grime from Joanna's face. "It is all right, *señora*. He is frightened for you." Consuelo spoke to her as if she were a child, stopping in the midst of her ministrations to gather Joanna's trembling frame into a motherly hug. "As soon as he sees you are all right, he will calm down," she assured her.

Joanna knew Consuelo was wrong, but she said nothing as she fought to suppress the dry, sobbing spasms in her chest.

What would happen now? she wondered anxiously. Wade would be all right; he'd sustained only a minor concussion and some very colorful bruises, Consuelo had told her. According to her, he'd staunchly refused to go to the hospital, so the doctor had reluctantly given in, on the condition that he be watched closely for the next twenty-four hours, and take it easy for the next few days.

The accident had clearly been Joanna's fault, and she felt smothered with guilt, even though Wade was not seriously hurt. If only she'd not gone charging blindly over that hill. A second sooner or a second later, and they would not have collided. Joanna shuddered again at the thought that they both could have been killed. Fortunately neither of their horses had been fatally injured, but both would require veterinary attention and several days' rest.

Joanna started at the knock on her door, pulling away from Consuelo as the woman called out for the doctor to enter. Joanna stoically endured Dr. Grant's examination of the swelling lump on her scalp, tensing against the pain as he gently checked her injured shoulder.

"I don't think there's anything broken," the young sandy-haired doctor reported, the smile he gave her taking some of the edge off the cold, sick tension in her middle. "But I'd like you and Wade to come to the clinic this week so I can see how you're getting along," he said as he helped her get her blouse back on. "In the meantime I want you to take it easy. You've taken a pretty hard tumble today. You'll probably be stiff and sore, so it might help to take a few warm baths and use a heating pad along with aspirin every four hours or so. Of course, if you become too uncomfortable and need something stronger before you can get to the office, give me a call." The doctor began to put away his stethoscope and Joanna finished buttoning her blouse.

"How is Wade?" she asked, hoping for more information than Consuelo had brought her earlier.

"Mild concussion, bruised ribs, sour disposition," he listed with a grin. "Nothing that a couple of days in bed won't help—that and knowing you're all right."

Joanna's gaze faltered, glad that Dr. Grant hadn't guessed the real truth—that Wade couldn't care less about her beyond the fact that she hadn't been seriously injured. From what she'd heard just a few minutes ago, Wade couldn't wait to get her in his room so he could give her the verbal upbraiding she deserved.

"Thank you, doctor," she said, managing a pale smile.

"You're welcome, Joanna. You take it easy for the next several days," he admonished gently. "And see that Wade does, too. Neither one of you have any business on a horse for at least a week."

"I will," she promised softly, and Dr. Grant walked to the door and stepped out. She listened as he moved down the hall toward Wade's room—to give him a report, she was certain.

Joanna rose stiffly from the side of the bed and went to her dresser to collect fresh underclothing. A few moments later she slipped beneath the shower, washing away the grime and letting the pulsing spray beat down soothingly on her injured shoulder. She was just getting into her thick terry robe, when Consuelo bustled into her room.

"Your husband is impatient to see you, *señora*. We are afraid that if you do not go in to him now, he will come after you."

"Please tell him I'd like to dry my hair first and get dressed," she said quietly, knowing she couldn't put off facing him much longer. The sooner she exposed herself to his anger, the sooner she could get it over with.

Consuelo rushed out, and Joanna dressed as quickly as possible. To her surprise, the woman came back just as she was finishing. "Perhaps you will let me help you with your hair, *señora*," she suggested.

"My, he really is impatient, isn't he?" she commented bitterly, trying to mask how much it hurt to know that Wade couldn't wait to vent his temper on her.

"He is impatient, *sí*," Consuelo said, the stern set to her face a very gentle reproach, "but I think your shoulder bothers you too much."

Joanna blushed, glancing away. She was sorry she'd jumped to the conclusion that Consuelo was more concerned with appeasing Wade's temper than she was with helping Joanna with what would now be a difficult task. After all, the woman was not a monster.

"I apologize, Consuelo. Yes, I could certainly use your help, if you wouldn't mind."

Consuelo smiled then, and proceeded to fuss over Joanna like a mother hen. Joanna sat quietly, her hysteria gone, basking in the care Consuelo gave her, until finally the simple chore was complete.

"Thank you very much, Consuelo," she said, then made her way reluctantly to Wade's door. She knocked softly on the dark wood and entered when he called out for her to come in.

Megan ceased her restless pacing between Wade's bedside and the balcony doors as Joanna stepped inside, but Joanna paid her little attention.

Wade lay propped against the carved wooden headboard of his bed with two thick pillows at his back. His boots and chaps and neckerchief had been removed, but he was still dressed in his jeans, his shirt pulled from the waistband and hanging open.

"I want to be alone with her, Meg," he growled, his eyes never leaving the uneasy pallor of Joanna's face. "I don't want anyone to bother us, hear?"

Joanna was sickened by his words and the almost angry way they were spoken. Megan left the room without comment, but flashed Joanna a sharp look on her way by. When the door closed, Joanna's heart seemed to rise into her throat.

"Are you feeling all right?" he asked.

"Yes. Are you?" she returned, her voice shaking with anxiety for him. The doctor had said he was in no danger, and she could see he looked very much like his vital self, but worry for him clung to her like a shroud. All she could think about were those awful, awful moments when she'd thought he might stop breathing.

"The doctor told me you've got a sore shoulder

and a nasty bump on your head. Are you sure you're feeling all right?'' he repeated, ignoring her question about him, the narrowed look he was giving her challenging the way she made light of her injuries.

"I'll be fine."

"Then come over here," Wade rasped, his face like granite, the gray cast to his skin replaced by a healthier, more natural color.

Joanna stepped to his bedside obediently, her anguished gaze searching his face for any sign of the pain she'd caused him. "I'm so sorry," she whispered, miserable with guilt, trying hard to restrain the tears that sparkled unshed.

Wade raised his hand toward her. "Give me your hand, Joanna," he growled, his eyes riveted to hers as if he could will her to put her small hand into his strong, rough grip.

Hesitantly, she reached for him, then found her slim, cold fingers swallowed up in the warmth of his. "You were right. It was dangerous for me to go with you today," she said. "I'm sorry I—"

"That's enough," Wade cut in, his soft drawl moving gently over her. The heat in his touch went directly to the cold knot in her middle and spread through it like warm honey. Joanna felt a little dizzy with confusion.

"But it was my fault," she insisted, biting her lip as her composure faltered. She felt a slight tug on her fingers and moved closer until her knee pressed against the mattress. When Wade started to pull her down beside him on the bed, she went rigid.

"Sit down here," he coaxed, then waited until Joanna gave in and perched herself gingerly on the edge of the bed. "Closer."

Joanna warily watched the softening expression on his face. "I don't understand what you want," she whispered, pain threading through her voice, clearly at a loss as to why he was behaving so strangely.

"I want you, Joanna," he rasped slowly, his thumb stroking over her sensitive inner wrist.

Joanna stared, unable to look away from the blue fire in his eyes as he drew her so close she was sitting at his hip. In the next moment, he was combing his fingers through her hair, curving them around the back of her neck. The light pressure he exerted made her sway toward him until their lips were little more than an inch apart.

"You did fine out there today. What happened was an accident." Joanna melted helplessly when he touched his lips tenderly to hers. "Just a case of bad timing," he rasped against her mouth, his breath mingling hotly with hers.

Joanna was on fire. Now that she knew what this unbearable tension and expectation building inside her could culminate in, she wanted it wildly. She didn't have the strength to resist him, and yet she had to.

Trembling, she started to withdraw, wincing as she put up a hand to the headboard to lever herself back. But the strong arms around her tightened and held her fast.

"I want to make love to you," Wade said bluntly,

the sensual intensity of his eyes streaking through her like lightning.

"But you've been hurt. You have a concussion," she reminded him, astonished that he could want her now.

"You've been hurt too, but we can be careful with each other," he whispered as he brushed his lips teasingly over hers, turning her insides to butter. "I want to have you."

Joanna's resistance scattered the instant Wade reached for the buttons of her blouse to escalate his sensual assault. Her eyes drifted closed when his fingers found the ultrasensitive swell of her breast. Slowly, carefully, he made love to her, and Joanna surrendered her body to his without a breath of protest.

CHAPTER TEN

"THE TWO OF YOU have been sleeping together, haven't you?" Megan accused, her lip curling back in disgust.

Joanna stood rigidly, facing Megan's fury with a calm that made Megan even angrier.

It was two and a half weeks since the accident. Joanna and Wade had spent only a few hours of that time alone with each other, but almost all of those had been spent in bed. Joanna had yet to actually sleep with Wade, since she always left him to return to her room once he fell asleep, but she knew exactly what Megan was asking and there was no way she could deny it.

"That's really none of your business," Joanna reminded her as she turned back to finish brushing Lucky before she put him into his stall. Joanna had done a bit more work on the range this morning than the day before, for the strained muscles in her shoulder and back were mending slowly, but it was the strange light-headedness she'd felt earlier that had warned her it might be wise to come back to the house. Perhaps it was still too soon after the accident for her to tolerate hard riding for any great length of time. Under the circumstances, she realized finally that she might not be up to putting in full days on the roundup for at least another week.

"You're making a fool of yourself," Megan taunted. "No woman with any self-respect would let herself be used as a substitute." She snickered.

Joanna released Lucky and closed the stall door, not allowing Megan to see how much her words distressed her. She might not have been bothered by them at all if Megan hadn't spoken aloud the very suspicions that had been tormenting her since the accident.

That was largely the reason she'd been working with an interior decorator the past two weeks in an effort to get the Double L ranch house in livable shape as soon as possible. The structural changes were already complete. The painters had started, and the carpet layers would begin after that.

She had been forced to acknowledge to herself that even though Wade knew of her demanding schedule to ready the ranch house, he had neither said nor done anything to dissuade her. In fact he hadn't remarked on it at all. Even in her most lovestruck state she had to admit that if he was in love with her, he would have had at least some questions about her haste to finish the remodeling work; she'd made it clear from the beginning that she would be living on the Double L by the time their divorce was final.

"Surely you didn't come back to the house early today just to cheer me up," Joanna pointed out with mild sarcasm.

Megan snorted inelegantly. "Hardly. I just thought I might have a better chance of talking to you alone."

"Are you finished?"

"For now," Megan allowed. The smug look on her face told Joanna that Megan was quite confident her mission had succeeded, and that if it hadn't, there would be more to come.

Joanna moved past her and walked through the barn, then on up to the house, her heart a turmoil of bittersweet emotion. Megan was probably right; she was just a substitute for Lorna Kemp. But Wade had such a convincing way of making her feel that it was she whom he loved. He'd never spoken the words, but when he held her in his arms she felt cherished, adored, loved. And when his lovemaking drove her over the edge of sanity, it was impossible to keep a steady grip on common sense.

Joanna entered the kitchen a few minutes later, and Consuelo turned from dinner preparations to greet her. "How was your morning, *señora*?" she asked, a cheerful smile lining her face with pleasant crinkles.

"It feels good to be out in the sunshine," Joanna said, then added wryly, "but only if the horse I'm on is moving slowly."

Consuelo laughed with her. "Perhaps you should not push yourself too quickly," she advised.

"I feel like a malingerer," Joanna said with a grimace. "Wade was back working the roundup almost right away, but I still can't seem to put in a full day, and it's been more than two weeks."

"But you do not have his constitution, *señora*, nor

his stubbornness, nor his hard head," Consuelo reminded her with a chuckle. "And, too, I do not think he will allow you to work too hard for many days yet."

"I have Dr. Grant to thank for that," Joanna murmured, still chafing a bit at what he'd told Wade when they'd gone in for their checkup at the clinic a few days after the accident. The doctor had convinced Wade that she might not be up to the strenuous work of the roundup for at least three more weeks. Though Wade had ignored Dr. Grant's advice for himself, he had been determined to enforce the doctor's advice for her, until Joanna had finally managed to persuade him to let her help out a little.

"You would do well to do as Dr. Grant says," Consuelo admonished gently. "He is a very good doctor."

"Mmm," Joanna responded noncommittally. Rarely ill, she wasn't accustomed to being restricted. Although she was indeed not ready for a full day of strenuous activity, she'd always made that kind of decision for herself. She wasn't sure she liked having someone make it for her. And in this case, it was possible to mistake Wade's caution as further evidence that he was in love with her, when he might be motivated solely by his relentless sense of responsibility, because of his agreement with her father.

"Is there something here I can help you with?" Joanna asked then, wanting to change the subject. She and Consuelo had become good friends since the accident and had spent a lot of pleasant, companionable time working together in the kitchen.

"Oh, no, *señora*. I am almost finished with everything," the woman told her, casually waving away her offer of assistance.

"When are you going to stop calling me that?" Joanna asked. "I thought we agreed you'd call me Joanna from now on."

Consuelo threw up her hands. "*Sí*, you are right, but it is hard to stop a habit...Joanna," she added with a smile.

"Thanks, Consuelo," she said softly. "If you don't need me for anything here, I've got some reading I should get finished." Consuelo nodded, and Joanna had just started for the den, when they heard the doorbell.

"I'll get it," Joanna called, then went to answer the front door.

"Mrs. Hollister?" The man she opened the door to was a small, balding man in his mid to late forties.

"Yes," she answered, immediately sensing the cold, officious formality in the man's manner, though he was dressed casually enough in jeans, sneakers and a white shirt.

"Mrs. Joanna Kay Lloyd Hollister?" he persisted.

"Yes," she repeated, wary now. "Is something wrong?"

"This should explain it all," he said, handing her a folded packet of papers, his distant manner sending a prickle of foreboding along her nerve endings as she reached for it.

"Good day, ma'am." The man turned, then walked briskly to his car.

A chill quivered down her spine and formed a sick weight in her stomach as she read her name on the packet. Stunned, feeling her senses reel and her vision swim as a wave of nausea washed over her, Joanna read the words that informed her that she was the respondent in the dissolution of her marriage.

SOMEHOW SHE MANAGED to eat the supper Consuelo had prepared; the fact that Wade was still out on the range helped. Megan ate with her, but to Joanna's relief, she did so without creating any of the unpleasantness that had marred many of their meals together when Wade was not there. When they were finished, Joanna slipped quietly up to her room, dealing with the shock by having a stern talk with herself.

She'd known all along this would happen. She'd even been the one to insist that Wade get things moving on their divorce before the start of roundup. It wasn't that she'd forgotten; it was more that she hadn't been expecting to be served the papers today. No, if she was honest with herself, she had to admit that some deep secret part of her had fallen into the trap of thinking that the past two and a half weeks really had somehow changed Wade's mind about the divorce.

But the signs had been there for days and she'd seen every one of them, knowing what they meant. It was her own fault if she'd allowed herself to cling to a last, irrational hope. After all, Wade had made no promises, no declarations of love.

She realized grimly that she wasn't quite strong enough to remain on the Ten Star. She could no more resist Wade than she could stop breathing, and Megan was right. No woman with any self-respect would allow herself to be used—especially when she had irrefutable proof that she was being discarded.

Joanna absently toyed with the tiny gold rose at her throat, until she realized what she was doing and reached up with trembling fingers to unclasp the chain. Wade had returned the necklace to her a few days ago, telling her he'd found it in his bed the morning after the barbecue, its frail chain broken. He'd sent it to San Antonio with Jake just before roundup to be repaired, and Jake had brought it back on the return trip.

He'd made no explanation for waiting those few days to give it back to her, and she hadn't asked; she'd been too stupidly thrilled to have it again. And of course, a moment later they were making love and she wouldn't have been able to put two intelligible words together if her life had depended on it.

A sick quiver went through her middle, and Joanna determinedly stemmed the tears that streaked silently down her cheeks. She had new plans to make, and she couldn't think clearly or carry them out if she indulged her feelings now. She had a lifetime for that.

THE NEXT MORNING, Joanna walked out of the Texas heat into the air-conditioned relief of Dr. Grant's small clinic in Ozona. Consuelo had mentioned earlier that she needed to go into town before lunch for a few supplies. Joanna had decided to take the opportunity to see Dr. Grant.

The nausea and light-headedness she'd been experiencing off and on for the past three days while riding hadn't concerned her much until last evening. It was then, during another bout of nausea, it dawned on her that the fatigue and queasiness she'd been feeling might not be related to the few hours a day she'd worked roundup since the accident.

The thought that she might be pregnant panicked her. Before she'd received the divorce papers, she might have been ecstatic at even the possibility of becoming pregnant. But now she'd had time to recall Wade's declaration weeks ago that any child of his by her would be his first heir and would remain on the Ten Star, she could feel little more than apprehension.

Joanna settled into one of the chairs in the waiting room and picked up a magazine, pretending interest in one of the articles until she realized her hands were shaking, and she impatiently thrust it aside.

She wanted to have Wade's child almost as much as she wanted his love, so perhaps the symptoms she'd been having were only the product of wishful thinking. Last night's bout of nausea might simply have been a nervous reaction to receiving the divorce papers. The other times could still have been the result of doing too much too quickly after the accident.

Joanna sat in an agony of worry as a bone-deep

weariness stole over her. She shifted uneasily, trying to throw off the tiredness by reminding herself she hadn't slept well last night. A light flush touched her cheeks as her mind went instantly to the reason.

She had been in the TV room upstairs, intending to wait until Wade had gone to bed and was asleep, before she went to her own room. She'd been too cowardly to acknowledge the receipt of the divorce papers to him and had elected to simply avoid him until she could get her things moved to the Double L.

But Wade had thwarted that plan by finding her and grabbing her up, smothering her startled protest with a ravenous kiss and he'd carried her down the hall to his bedroom and kicked the door closed.

Her resistance to him had been shamefully short-lived. Inwardly she cringed as she remembered how easily she'd given in to his lovemaking. He'd barely allowed her time to take a breath, much less refuse him. He'd chuckled at her initial attempts to wiggle out of his arms and, as if he thought it a variation of their love play, he'd escalated his tender assault and she'd melted away into mindlessness. Later, she'd lain awake half the night, savoring the feel of his sleep-weighted arm across her, yet hating herself for being so vulnerable to a man who apparently had no scruples about making love to a woman he was soon to divorce.

Tears of impotence blurred her vision. She'd been too weak, too in love with him to manage more than what now seemed to be only a halfhearted attempt to resist him.

Knowing how susceptible she was made it imperative that she leave the Ten Star, but the house at the Double L still wasn't quite finished enough to be lived in. The contractor had assured her this morning she could move into it in a couple more days, but Joanna doubted she could wait that long.

"Mrs. Hollister?"

Joanna glanced up, grateful to be distracted from her thoughts. She stood quickly to follow the nurse to the examining room, her heart a turmoil of dread and hope.

Hours later, Dr. Grant called her himself with the results of the blood test. He'd seemed a little confused when Joanna requested he keep the results confidential until she notified him otherwise, but he'd agreed to do so. For as long as she could manage it—at least until the divorce was final—she and Dr. Grant would be the only ones who knew that Wade Hollister had fathered his first heir.

"*SEÑORA*—JOANNA—please reconsider what you are doing," Consuelo pleaded as Joanna swung the small suitcase into the trunk of Megan's car, then stepped aside for Megan to toss in the last one.

"I have, Consuelo." Joanna turned to the Mexican woman, stretching her pale lips into a half smile. "This is the way it was supposed to be from the beginning."

"But Joanna..." Consuelo's voice faded away

when Joanna's expression became a sober mask and her hazel eyes turned distant.

"I hope you'll come visit, Consuelo. You've been a good friend to me," Joanna said, her brisk tone of voice concealing the wild tumble of emotions that had given her no rest since she'd received the divorce papers and learned she was pregnant, then been forced to wait another week to leave the Ten Star. Her house was now finished enough for her to live in it, and Wade was gone, deeply involved with the roundup and not expected back until nightfall. Joanna had begged off going with him that day with the excuse of having to oversee the contractors in the final stages of their work.

The wait had been almost more than she could stand. She had kept the delivery of the divorce papers to herself and had avoided Wade while having to cope with delay after delay with the contractors.

Fortunately he had camped out several nights with his men, and though she'd declined his many invitations to spend the night with him at the campsite, she hadn't been able to resist him on the nights he'd spent at the ranch house. No matter what ploy she used to distance herself from him, he'd always managed to slip past her defenses and make her forget everything but those earthshaking moments in his arms.

The hardest part of those nights had come after he fell asleep, leaving her awake to struggle with her conscience and to chastise herself for her cowardice and her weakness.

But now she was leaving at last, aided and abetted

by a delighted Megan. Megan had been quite civil and very helpful once Joanna had explained her intention to leave Wade and move to the Double L. Megan had even offered to come back to the house from roundup at midmorning just to give her a ride over.

Joanna returned the quick impulsive hug Consuelo gave her, then hurried to get into the passenger seat of Megan's little blue car.

"You're doing the right thing," Megan said once they reached the highway and she'd accelerated blithely past the speed limit. Joanna didn't respond, staring straight through the windshield, feeling the faint stirring in her middle that signaled the onset of one of the bouts of nausea that had plagued her for the past week and a half. She'd planned on making the trip with Megan that morning so she could be safely moved by afternoon, but Megan's tardy arrival had prevented that.

Joanna clenched her fists and gritted her teeth, praying Megan would be as self-centered as usual and not notice anything was wrong. In the end, though, Joanna's discomfort increased until she couldn't wait another mile and was forced to ask Megan to stop the car.

The vehicle had barely stopped moving when Joanna opened the door and put a foot on the ground, prepared to stagger clear in case she actually did lose her lunch. Somehow she managed not to be sick, and Megan waited in total silence until Joanna pulled her foot back in the car and closed the door, leaning her head back wearily against the seat.

"My God, you aren't…?" Megan was shaking her head. "You can't be…pregnant," she whined in disbelief.

Joanna turned her head slightly to look over at her sister-in-law's stunned expression. "Let that be a lesson to you, Megan," she joked weakly. "The only sure method of birth control is celibacy."

Megan banged a small fist against the steering wheel. "You aren't going to use this to trap Wade," she declared.

"That's right. Wade won't know anything about it until our divorce is final," Joanna said, then closed her eyes. "I'm not about to trap him." She smiled bitterly. "Who knows? By the time he finds out, he might be persuaded to think the child is someone else's." After all, she wasn't more than three and a half weeks along.

Megan was silent for a moment. "Not Jake's!" she shrilled. "You're not going to even hint that it's his!"

Joanna sighed, then shook her head. "Why would I do something like that? Jake's all yours, Megan, if he'll have you. Wade's the only man I want, but he's not in love with me." Joanna opened her eyes and looked over at Megan's skeptical expression. "Relax. I'm leaving Wade, and I won't tell him about the baby. I may even find an apartment in San Angelo or San Antonio before I begin to show so he won't find out until after it's born."

Megan was watching her warily now. "I don't understand. You have the perfect weapon. Wade would never let you leave if he knew you were pregnant. He would probably even be foolish enough to stay married to you and let you stay on the Ten Star to help raise the child, as long as the two of you got along.'' Megan was shaking her head and her eyes were narrowed, as if she was searching for some shadowy ulterior motive.

"That's the difference between the way you and I think, Megan. I love Wade enough to want his happiness, even though it means he might only be happy with Lorna.'' Joanna stopped, but not quickly enough to catch the sob that slipped out unexpectedly, or the disheartened tear that shot down her cheek. She saw no reason not to tell Megan the truth about her love for Wade, because she knew it was a secret Megan would guard faithfully.

"But I'm not making any noble sacrifice, you understand,'' Joanna said with a sniffle, a watery smile on her lips. "I just know that if I used this baby to shackle him to me so he'd have to give up Lorna again, eventually he'd grow to hate the sight of me. Maybe he'd hate the child, too.''

"Wade wouldn't hate any child,'' Megan piped up, a strange look on her face as she stared over at Joanna.

Joanna glanced away, impatiently brushing the tear trail from her cheek. "He might not,'' she conceded, then stated with certainty, "but you would. I shudder to think what torments you could devise, and the effect they would have on an innocent child.''

"I—I wouldn't," Megan gasped. Joanna was sur-prised by the shock and distress on Megan's face. "I wouldn't harm a child."

"Maybe not Wade's child," Joanna agreed, "but the child would also be half-mine, of my body. And if it had the misfortune to resemble me in any way, I think you could be positively cold-blooded."

Megan was livid with outrage, and Joanna noticed that her hands were shaking. "I would never, ever, do that to a child," Megan said, her eyes blazing with resentment.

"How am I supposed to know that?" Joanna chal-lenged. "I don't have a crystal ball to see into the future, and I certainly can't read your mind. I can only go by the way you've acted toward me, and judging from that, I can only conclude that you're capable of almost anything."

Megan turned her face away abruptly, clenching and unclenching her hands on the steering wheel. It was several moments before she reached out to put the car in gear and continue down the road to the Double L.

Joanna hadn't expected to hear from Wade that first day, and was quite unprepared to have her seven-o'clock breakfast disrupted the next morning.

"Have you got a reason for walking out on me?" Wade demanded as he shoved aside the screen of the patio door and stepped uninvited into her kitchen. Joanna jerked in surprise, spilling a few drops of cof-fee into her lap. She jumped to her feet, setting her coffee down with one hand, while she whisked the hot spots away with the other.

"Have you got a reason for barging into my home without my consent?" she retaliated, clutching quickly for the protection of anger to conceal her weakness at the mere sight of him. It had been only a little more than twenty-four hours, but already she missed him desperately.

"I'm your husband," he growled.

"Is that supposed to excuse your behavior?" She reached for a dishcloth to blot up the spilled coffee on the tabletop.

"It should entitle me to a few privileges, yes," he asserted.

"Well, in case it escaped your notice, you and I are now separated. That means your privileges as a husband have been suspended," she informed him, taking more time than the chore warranted as she gathered up her breakfast dishes.

"Why, Joanna?"

Joanna felt herself falter at the husky timbre of his voice. But when she looked up to meet the iron quality in his gaze, she gave every impression of being aloof, utterly removed from him, her serenity projecting an eerie calm, which gave credence to what she would say.

"I couldn't live with you anymore," she confessed. That much was the truth. "Under the circumstances it seemed quite immoral to me for things to go on the way they had been, when we both knew it was just sex. I always felt cheap the next day." Joanna's gaze fell from his, a genuine feeling of humiliation masking the lie. It still unsettled her that he could so easily strip her inhibition and turn her into a mindless, writhing wanton.

"Was it just sex?"

Joanna didn't dare look up, her lowered lashes hiding the anguish that twisted her insides. She abruptly turned to place her dishes in the dishwasher.

"Do you think for a moment I would have left you if I were in love with you?" she asked, taking great care to place the dishes just so in the rack. "I left because I couldn't think of any easy way to end the relationship," she added briskly. "I hardly expected you'd come charging over here and embarrass us both."

"What day did they serve you with the divorce papers?" he demanded then, correctly guessing they were the reason she'd left him.

"That has very little to do with why I left you, Wade," she lied. "And I've already explained my reasons."

"I asked you what day they served you with the papers," he snapped.

Joanna stiffened and turned to face him. "The papers were delivered a few days ago. Just over a week, since you're so determined to know."

"Why didn't you tell me you'd got them?"

"You knew they were coming," she reminded him. "Surely your lawyer gave you some idea when I would be receiving them."

Wade was watching her closely. "Maybe I should

ask you why you stayed around this past week if you'd already been served with the papers," he said, his eyes narrowing slyly. It was a look that gave him a dangerous, lying-in-wait appearance, and warned her he could be a hard-bitten, formidable man, one not easily fooled.

"I had to wait until this house was finished enough to live in it," she answered, thankful that she had a plausible excuse. The way Wade looked, he was determined to get an answer out of her. "And since I'm not able to drive a car yet, I couldn't just climb in one and take off. It took some time to get everything in order."

"And in the meantime, you never turned me down, never hinted that our sexual relationship bothered you in the least." Wade's mouth slanted bitterly. "You'll pardon me if I find that hard to believe," he mocked, relentlessly pushing closer to whatever he was trying to get her to admit.

Joanna's face flamed. "You underestimate your... expertise," she said, her eyes sliding away from his as she turned her back, unable to think of anything else to say that would throw him off the track he seemed to be taking. Was he trying to get a confession of love from her? she wondered frantically. She couldn't bear to have him find out. "And, as I recall, whenever you did come in from roundup, we never spent a lot of time talking."

"Consuelo mentioned you'd been to Dr. Grant's office a few days ago. Was it because you're still having a little trouble with your shoulder, or are you pregnant?''

Joanna was glad he couldn't see her face. "You've taken birth-control precautions these past weeks," she evaded. "You should know the answer to that."

"We didn't that first night, or the night of the accident," he reminded her harshly, "and it's been a little under a month since the accident."

"Everything is normal. You have nothing to worry about," she said hastily before he could pose a yes or no question to her again.

Technically both statements were true. Everything was normal for a woman who'd conceived and was now in the very early stages of pregnancy. And Wade had nothing to worry about. She wouldn't use a baby to keep him, or to extort anything from him, or to harm his second chance with Lorna. The child would live with her and be her responsibility.

"Well then," he said after a lengthy, charged silence, "I reckon if there's no baby, and nothing between us but good sex that makes you feel cheap, there's not much reason for you and me to be living together under the same roof. That right?"

Joanna took a slow, silently agonized breath and nodded.

"You've got a good foreman in Bill Black," he continued. "I figure you might be ready to start taking over the Double L on your own, so we'll give it a trial. I'll be around now and then to check up on things, unless you run into problems in the meantime.

If that happens, don't be too proud to call. I still owe your father.''

Tears brimmed in Joanna's eyes as she listened to Wade walk to the patio door, slide it open and step outside. The screen panel hissed closed with a snap. Only when she heard the sound of his boots as he walked away did she turn and hurry to a window to discreetly watch him go.

He hadn't come after her to make any confessions of undying love. Instead he'd wanted to know why she'd left him and if she was pregnant. She guessed now that he'd been more upset because he'd lost a sexual convenience than because she'd walked out on him. He'd not once hinted that he wanted her back, hadn't even suggested that their relationship might continue as it had by offering her a plausible reason for having sex for sex' sake.

And that only proved that he could find the kind of sexual relationship he'd had with her with anyone, that he wasn't going to put himself to any real bother to keep her when any woman would do. She knew he was counting the days until the divorce was final and he was at long last free to court Lorna. Joanna tried not to think about how much that hurt.

She lived reclusively for the next several weeks, going out daily to watch the progress of the Double L roundup, but never participating. The barn was being rebuilt, the house was finished, and she'd at last got everything situated just the way she wanted it.

It was a hot, breezy day in late June when she heard

from one of the Hollisters, and then it was Megan who came calling.

Joanna was sitting in the lounger on her new patio, but didn't bother to get up when she saw who it was. She'd felt wrung out all day, abnormally weak and tired, until every expenditure of energy seemed to cost her. Sitting in the shade with her feet up might have been the perfect cure, but thanks to the backache that was plaguing her that afternoon, she couldn't quite manage to get comfortable.

In the past few minutes, she'd experienced a couple of sharp abdominal cramps, but had dismissed them. She'd had them a day or so before, too, but the cramps had stopped by the time she got back to the house and could call the doctor. She'd figured she'd just been riding too much. She was due for a prenatal checkup later in the week and had decided to wait and report the cramps to the doctor then. With any luck, she thought, Megan wouldn't stay long. She just didn't feel up to the kind of discussion she and Megan usually had.

"I was wondering if we could have a talk," Megan began.

Joanna was suddenly aware that there was something different in Megan's manner. "I guess that depends on what you want to talk about," she returned coolly.

Megan's gaze fell guiltily from hers. "I've been thinking a lot about what you said the day I brought you over here," she murmured. "My conscience has bothered me ever since then. And if you wouldn't mind I'd like to explain...and apologize.''

Joanna couldn't help but stare. Megan was behaving strangely; she had never seen her like this. The saucy, spiteful arrogance she had come to expect seemed remarkably absent in Megan now. She realized she was seeing a side of the other woman that she hadn't suspected was there. For some reason, too, Joanna didn't doubt for a moment that what she sensed was genuine.

''Go ahead and sit down,'' she invited, curious, watching intently as Megan dragged a patio chair closer and perched stiffly on its edge.

''It might help if I could explain a few things,'' Megan began hesitantly.

''It might,'' Joanna agreed, unsure of Megan's reason for coming here and where this was all leading.

''I've been in love with Jake Terrell for ages—ever since I was eleven or twelve,'' Megan stated, not able to maintain eye contact with Joanna for more than a moment at a time. She paused and shifted uncomfortably.

While Megan was searching for the right words, Joanna suddenly felt a sharp, knife blade of pain rip through her abdomen. Megan's eyes had been avoiding hers for those long seconds, so Joanna was able to regain control over her facial reaction and conceal what had just happened by the time Megan looked her way. When the cramp finally eased, Joanna's strength seemed to ebb with it.

''What's that got to do with what I said that day?''

Joanna prompted. Alarm made her suddenly impatient for Megan to come to the point and leave, so she could call one of the ranch hands up from the barn to drive her to the doctor. There was something terribly wrong inside her; her every instinct was telling her so.

Megan seemed a bit surprised at Joanna's impatience, but she took a deep breath and rushed on obligingly, uncharacteristically willing to please. "When you said you thought I could hate a child because it was yours, and that you believed I was capable of tormenting it, I took a long hard look at myself." Megan's face flushed.

"I was jealous, Joanna. I wanted Wade to divorce you so he could distract Lorna from some of the attention Jake had started showing her whenever he was unhappy with me. Until the day you stepped onto the Ten Star, I'd taken for granted that Wade and Lorna would get together, and everything with me and Jake would fall into place." Megan's lips formed a crooked line as she paused, giving Joanna a moment to digest her words.

"Looking back now, it all seems incredibly selfish and petty. I think I've finally come to the realization that if Jake isn't going to fall in love with me, then manipulating everyone else isn't going to win him, either."

Megan met Joanna's watchful gaze with solemn eyes. "I sincerely wish I could go back to that first day when you climbed out of the plane and start again. I realize now just how cruel I was to you. I know you don't have much use for my friendship, and I can't blame you, but I just had to come over here and talk to you. I apologize, Joanna.''

Joanna had gone deathly white, her lips parted on a gasp of pain as she clutched her stomach. Megan was on her knees beside her in an instant.

"What's wrong? Is it the baby?" she asked anxiously.

The cramp eased enough for Joanna to catch her breath and nod. "I need to get to a doctor," she panted, her eyes huge with fright as she slid her legs off the side of the lounger and tried to get up. "Will you call one of the men to drive me in to Ozona?"

"I'll take you," Megan said, reaching to help her to her feet. "But the hospital at Ozona will probably send you on to one in San Angelo for this. I'll get you to my car, then I'll make a quick call to Dr. Grant to see what he says."

Joanna felt worse as she walked to the car. Her legs were trembling by the time Megan got the door open and helped her in. Once Joanna was settled, Megan dashed back to the house. She raced out again a few minutes later and got behind the wheel.

"Please hurry," Joanna told her, feeling the onset of another severe cramp as Megan started the car. "I think I'm going to lose the baby," she whispered, the anguish in her heart growing more unbearable by the moment.

"Hang on," Megan urged as she jammed down on the accelerator and sent the little blue sports car rocketing down the drive. "Wade flew up to Dallas this morning, but we're going to meet Jake at the Little Mesquite airstrip and he'll fly you to San Angelo. He'll get you there in time.''

Joanna dropped her head back and closed her eyes, panting miserably with pain as she prayed for the car to go faster.

When they arrived at the airstrip, Lorna was waiting with Jake. Megan stayed only long enough to help them get Joanna into the plane, then she stepped back to her car, a sad look of resignation on her face as she watched Lorna strap herself in beside Joanna.

Jake started the engine and flew them to the airport at San Angelo, but it was already too late by the time he lifted Joanna from the seat of the small aircraft and handed her down to the ambulance attendants.

The miscarriage had happened much too quickly. With shocking clarity, Joanna had felt the tiny unborn life slip from her body's grasp, and she'd reeled beneath the double blow of guilt and grief. It was a bitter, wounding loss for her, one that somehow resurrected and underscored a lifetime of other losses— her mother, her father, Wade....

CHAPTER ELEVEN

"WADE'S OUTSIDE," Lorna said as she watched Joanna's back.

Joanna stiffened. "I asked you not to call him," she rasped crossly. "I don't want to see him." She was standing at the hospital window, pretending interest in the midmorning skyline of San Angelo while she waited for a nurse to bring a wheelchair. The doctor had just released her after her routine overnight hospital stay following the miscarriage, and Joanna was impatient to leave.

"He wants to see you, honey," Jake said. "He would have been here sooner if we'd been able to track him down."

"I don't want to see him," she repeated. "I don't want to see anyone." She turned angry, tear-bruised eyes to the gentle look Jake was giving her. "I want to be by myself. Why can't you understand that?" she snapped.

Jake seemed unaffected by her outburst. "The last thing you need right now is to be alone," he said, his drawl low and gravelly and slow. The sound of it soothed her ragged emotions like a comforting balm, making her ache to stop struggling against the tired lethargy that still clung to her. Her eyes felt heavy and raw, and all she wanted to do was close them and sleep. "Come on, honey," he coaxed. "Wade's out there fit to be tied."

A defeated sob jerked through her frame, and Joanna felt a fresh sting of tears. The doctor had warned her about the emotional roller coaster she would be on for a while, likening it to the postpartum blues many women experienced after the birth of a child. But nothing had quite prepared her for the dark depth of the depression she felt. If only she'd taken the cramping seriously and gone to the doctor right away, she'd agonized over and over. But it was too late, the child was gone, and Joanna was eaten alive with grief and guilt.

And now she had to face Wade, whether she wanted to or not, at just the time when her control over her emotions was as tenuous as rotted thread. It took every bit of strength she had to suppress the compelling urge to burst into tears, but somehow she managed to find it, finally able to nod her consent for Wade to come in.

Jake and Lorna stepped out into the hall. Joanna listened to the soft murmur of voices as the door closed, waiting in agonized suspense when several moments passed and Wade didn't appear. When the door finally did open, she heard the soft scuff of boots as he stepped inside, then paused, letting the door swish shut.

An incredible tingling sensation spiraled over her from head to toe, stirring her low spirits from the tomblike pit they'd been cast into, but Joanna didn't turn or acknowledge Wade in any way.

"I'm sorry I couldn't get here sooner," he said gruffly.

Joanna shrugged. "You didn't have to interrupt your trip to Dallas," she told him, her voice thin and brittle. "There was nothing you could have done anyway."

"Maybe not," he agreed. "Are you all right?"

Joanna nodded, choking back the tears that rushed against her frail control.

An awkward silence filled the room. The doctor had explained that it might take some time to recover her strength, but Joanna realized, with some dismay, that her legs were already beginning to weaken. She guessed Wade was standing between her and the bed, but even if she turned to go to the chair, she'd have to look at him.

And that was the problem. Ridiculous as it was, something told her that if she looked at him, her control might shatter and she'd break down. Not for anything did she want him to feel sorry for her, and tears—especially the huge, drowning ones she was fighting to restrain—would have her in his arms in a second and create a multitude of new problems for them both. She had a terrible, terrible fear that they would both mistake pity for love.

"Why don't you sit down?" Wade suggested gently. Joanna shook her head, waiting stoically for the nurse to come with the wheelchair to whisk her out of this room and away from Wade.

She tensed as she heard Wade walk over to join her at the window, sensing at the last moment that he was going to touch her. Warm strong hands closed caressingly over her shoulders, and the first soul-deep consolation she'd been able to feel began to trickle over her.

With the slightest of pressure, he turned her to face him, and Joanna hesitated, her eyes downcast. She couldn't bear to look at him, but once her eyes came up and made contact, she couldn't seem to pull them away.

As usual Wade looked as if he'd just ridden in from the range and stepped down off his horse. He bore no traces of the sweat and grime that went with cowboying, since he'd just got off a plane, but the sight of his lean, rawhide-tough masculinity stunned her into realizing just how hungry she'd been for even a glimpse of him.

The scent of his after-shave assailed her nostrils, calling up the scents of leather and sunshine and outdoors, and it was all she could do not to fling herself into his arms and bury her face against his chest. The tears were suddenly so thick in her throat that she couldn't have said anything if her life had depended on it.

Slowly he lowered his head, pausing to press a kiss to her forehead before his lips touched hers, the simple, exquisitely tender kiss easing its warmth and compassion into the fresh wound in her heart. It was when Wade ended that kiss, then bent again to deliver the unrestrained heat of the next, that Joanna managed to turn her face and pull away, her heart pounding from the torture of denying herself what she wanted most in the world.

"Please…stop," she cried hoarsely. All at once, the chaos of raw emotion she'd worked so hard to repress came roiling up, and she fled into the hall.

"Jake, I can't wait," she said as she clutched his arm, desperate to leave, her face strained and pale, the violet smudges of weariness beneath her eyes deeper than ever.

Jake's dark gaze lifted from her to focus over her head, turning hard and accusing as it raked Wade's face. "Sure, darlin'," he said, his eyes still locked in a silent duel with Wade's as he wrapped his arm around Joanna's shoulders and drew her protectively against his side. "You coming with us, Lorna?" he asked as he looked over to Lorna.

Lorna glanced worriedly from one man to the other, then silently shook her head.

"Talk to you later, then," he mumbled as he and Joanna started down the hall, the easy strength of his body supporting the trembling weakness of her own.

Luckily Jake didn't protest too vigorously when she insisted on returning to the Double L that day. She found out why when Lorna appeared at her door later, a suitcase in her hand. Though Joanna managed to conceal most of her melancholy from Jake and Lorna, both of them hovered over her, refusing to allow her to spend those first few days alone.

Consuelo insisted on deluging them with special meals, and Jake visited almost daily, but at Joanna's

request, Wade stayed away. She was convinced she
needed to maintain an emotional distance from him,
a distance she'd already discovered would be impossible to keep if she had to see him when she felt so
vulnerable.

Gradually her grief began to subside, and as she
began to regain most of her strength, she was able to
put her feelings of guilt into perspective. The doctor
at San Angelo had told her that there had been no
chance to prevent the miscarriage. The onset had been
too sudden, even if she had been able to get to a
doctor immediately. Some things were just not to be,
he'd counseled, and now Joanna was in a better frame
of mind to accept that.

Lorna moved back to her ranch, finally convinced
that Joanna was recovering, and Joanna was genuinely sorry to see her go. Lorna had helped her past
the worst of her grief, and Joanna felt she had made
a close friend.

And somewhere along the line, Lorna seemed to
have stopped mourning the loss of her husband.
Though Jake wasn't so sure, it was quite clear to
Joanna. At least something good had come out of the
ordeal of the past few days, and Joanna took it as a
sign that there was still happiness to be had in the
world.

"THE TWO OF YOU must've bought out every boutique
in San Antone," Jake chuckled. He groaned as Lorna
added another package to the precarious stack of
boxes and shopping bags he had been wrestling with

for the past hour. Joanna's purchases fitted neatly enough into the three shopping bags she carried, so she could manage easily on her own.

"We left at least a couple of shopping malls for tomorrow," Lorna joked, and Jake grunted, playfully complaining that his boots were made for stirrups, not for stomping around in shopping malls.

"Last time I let myself get set up to fly two shopaholics to town," he muttered, but the twinkle in his eye suggested he'd do it again.

Joanna smiled as she listened to Jake and Lorna's banter, happy that the friendship between the two had grown increasingly more affectionate these past few weeks, but surprised it hadn't developed into something more serious yet. And, if she were honest with herself, she had to admit she was deeply disappointed it hadn't.

Selfishly she realized that if Jake and Lorna remained only friends, Wade still had a better than even chance to win Lorna. The thought depressed her. Their divorce should soon be final, and Wade would at last be free to pursue the woman he'd had to give up to marry Joanna. And though Joanna loved Wade and valued Lorna's friendship enough to want them to be happy, she couldn't help the secret jealousy she felt, or the fear she had of facing a future as loveless as her past, forever hankering after the man she could never have.

"What a faker you are, Jake Terrell," Lorna scolded, distracting Joanna from her unhappy thoughts. "I saw the way you lit up when we went into that lingerie shop."

A sheepish smile curved one side of Jake's mouth. "Now I didn't say I was miserable the whole time," he admitted. "It ain't often us hardworkin' ol' boys get a treat like that one."

Lorna and Joanna giggled.

"Is that right?" Lorna responded, fixing her gaze a bit more intently than usual on Jake's as her smile faded slightly and a silent message shot from her eyes to his.

"That's a fact, ma'am," Jake drawled slowly, the sudden seriousness on his face communicating a message of its own.

Joanna would have had to be blind not to see the awareness that passed between them for those few seconds before Lorna abruptly changed the subject.

"I think Joanna and I would like to get upstairs and slip into a nice hot bath before we treat you to an expensive dinner."

Jake seemed a little slower to recover, but when he did, he grimaced. "Fancy hotels, designer clothes and expensive dinners. Sounds like I'm in the company of a pair of women who have some awfully high-priced notions. Might be a little rich for this simple cowpoke's blood."

Lorna grinned. "It's a good thing you aren't as simple as you like to let on." With that, she turned and led the way to the bank of elevators, punching the button for their floor when the three of them stepped inside one.

Joanna let herself into her room, closing the door behind her, hearing the satisfying click when it automatically locked. She walked to the closet in the dim room and set her purchases inside, pausing to take out the pink silk-and-satin teddy she'd bought on impulse when Lorna had selected several pieces of seductive lingerie for herself.

It had been a silly waste of money, since she'd never wear it, but she couldn't help getting a little caught up in Lorna's shopping enthusiasm. Lorna had confided that this was the first big shopping trip she'd been on since her husband's death, and that she was ready to pull out all the stops. Joanna had been more than ready herself for a little extravagance to lift her own spirits, and had somehow become daring enough during their spree to buy something with a man's pleasure in mind. Wade's pleasure.

The thought brought a wistful curve to her lips as she carefully folded the slippery fabric and started to place it back into the sack. Then, reconsidering, she took out the teddy, and turned toward the bathroom for her bath.

The moment Joanna stepped from the bathroom, she detected a subtle difference in the very air of her room. Perhaps it was the teddy, she thought as she looked down at it, fingering the thin, satiny bow of the drawstring that ribboned the waist.

She had just switched off the bathroom light and walked around the short wall that divided the closet and bathroom from the bedroom, when she froze.

Sitting on the bed with his booted feet up, his back

against the headboard—looking for all the world as if he belonged there—was Wade. Shock sent her blood pounding wildly through her body, and she couldn't have fled to find her robe or taken cover to save her life.

Blue eyes smoky with desire moved over her, the blatant sexual intent she read in their depths turning her insides to hot liquid.

The look she was giving him was just as intent, just as filled with desire, as her eyes scanned the length of the long, hard body that lay on the coverlet, sweeping over his wide shoulders and chest, dropping to find their way down his lean middle to his silver belt buckle, lingering with unconscious length at the way his jeans snuggled against his masculinity and hugged his muscular thighs.

Anticipation lent blooms of color to her cheeks as her hazel eyes tracked slowly back to his face. She was aching with the awareness that he was as handsome as ever, when her gaze connected with his and excitement shimmered between them.

"How did you get in?" she whispered, dismayed that she seemed to have lost her voice.

"Jake and Lorna made sure the room reservations were made in both our names so I'd have a key," he said, gesturing to indicate the room key he'd tossed on the dresser, as he swung his long legs off the edge of the mattress and came to his feet.

Joanna shook her head slightly. "They did that?"

Wade nodded, his eyes dropping to the soft round

thrust of her breasts against the pink satin as he walked toward her. "I asked them to."

Joanna made a self-conscious movement to cover herself. "I have to get my ro—"

"Please don't, Joanna," he rasped, his eyes coming up to look her full in the face. "I'd stare at you anyway. Any man would, if he was as starved for you as I am."

Joanna's heart twisted. "That's just a line," she whispered, unable to keep the fine tremors of pain from her voice. "A line a handsome man feeds to a woman he thinks is desperate to feel wanted," she said bitterly, anger sparkling in her eyes as she added, "so he can use her."

"If I wanted to use a woman, there are any number of women who could take care of me," he pointed out bluntly, his hands raising to rest cockily on his trim hips. "And none of them would expect the kind of emotional obligations and complications you do."

"Then you're welcome to go find one," she said as she turned and walked to her closet. She fetched her robe, then belted it securely around herself. She was just about to close the closet door, when she noticed the extra suitcase on the floor beneath the luggage rack that held hers.

"What's this doing in here?" she demanded as she leaned down to heft it out.

"Leave it be, Joanna," he ordered. "And come here."

Joanna straightened, electing to leave his suitcase where it was. She had little choice. Even if she managed to toss it out, she could hardly toss him out with it. Her only course was either to persuade him to leave, or to leave herself.

"What do you want?" she asked, not looking his way at all.

"To talk," he answered simply. "First."

"Talk is all you'll have," she answered, flashing him a defiant look. "First and last."

"All right," he conceded with suspicious ease, waiting until Joanna stepped a bit closer. "For now."

"What do you want to talk about?" she prompted, eager to get this over with. Her determination to resist him was almost nonexistent, and she was upset by the knowledge that it would take little or no effort on his part to get what he was hinting he wanted from her.

"Have you...recovered?" he asked.

Joanna had to look away from the concern that came into his eyes. "Yes," she answered, relaxing a bit. She walked farther into the bedroom, but kept a prudent distance from Wade and the bed.

"Why didn't you tell me the truth about your pregnancy? You had to have known, or at least guessed, by the time I asked you about it," he said sternly.

Joanna smoothed a hand down the soft cotton of her robe, not looking at him. "I didn't want you to feel trapped. You might have insisted we stay married...or kept the baby and driven me away." Tears she thought had stopped weeks ago suddenly crowded into her downcast eyes.

"You didn't expect much from me, did you?" It

was an accusation. Joanna shook her head, blinking a couple of times to restrain her tears.

"It's best not to expect a lot. My father taught me that," she murmured, lifting her chin.

Wade was silent for a long time.

"Your father didn't know the first thing about raising a little girl, and he was afraid to try," he began, suddenly shifting the direction the conversation was taking by responding to her comment about Will. "That's why he sent you away to your aunt to raise."

Taken aback by Wade's quick change of subject, Joanna's eyes flew to his.

"He made a lot of mistakes with you, Joanna, but he made most of them because he had no idea how to raise you without your mother's guidance." Wade's stern expression eased a little. "William Lloyd was as tough as boot leather, knew everything about ranching and how to handle his men, but dealing with his own daughter scared the daylights out of him."

Joanna couldn't help the spurt of resentment she felt. "He could have hired someone to take care of me," she pointed out stubbornly.

"He could have," Wade agreed, "but he didn't. The point is, are you going to let the mistakes your old man made with you influence the way you see yourself and how you interpret everyone else's actions for the rest of your life?"

A little stunned by Wade's question, Joanna didn't know how to respond. Her mind was whirling.

"Because I'll tell you something," he said as he

took a step closer to her, "whatever your father's motivation was for marrying you off to me, as it turned out, marrying you was the best thing that could have happened to me at the time. It kept me from making the mistake of marrying Lorna."

Joanna was dumbfounded. "What?"

"You heard me. Marrying Lorna would have been a big mistake." Wade watched a tiny glimmer of hope mingle with the skepticism in Joanna's eyes, and he waited a moment to let the words sink in before he went on, his voice softer.

"I wouldn't have made love to you, Joanna, unless I had some very deep feelings for you," he drawled, his voice a husky rasp as he spoke directly to her doubt. Joanna continued to watch him warily. "And if I'd been as in love with Lorna as I am with you, nothing you could have done would have got me into that bed with you."

Wade's big hand extended toward her, and she automatically started to reach for it before she hesitated, then resolutely kept her hand clenched at her side.

He wasn't really saying what she thought he was, she warned herself. He couldn't possibly be saying he loved her. Somehow he knew how to say all the right things, just as he'd known how to do all the right things those times they'd made love. As much as she wanted to believe him, she couldn't allow herself to. Her heart would be damaged beyond recovery this time. She couldn't take another loss.

"You were probably just..." Joanna shrugged. "You'd waited for Lorna a long time."

Wade suddenly grinned. "You think I used you to soothe my sexual frustration over Lorna?" he concluded with a chuckle, and Joanna's face went red with humiliation. "Wasn't it at least a remote possibility that I made love with you so I could soothe the sexual frustrations you caused?"

Joanna shook her head, not trusting herself to speak. He was making fun of her.

Wade's gaze moved over her shamed expression, fastening on the deep well of hurt in her eyes. "Oh, hell, Joanna," he rumbled, then closed the space between them and took her fiercely into his arms. Joanna struggled against him, but Wade easily subdued her attempt to wiggle out of his embrace while he quickly dispensed with her robe.

"Feel what you do to me," he demanded as his hand slipped down to her rounded backside and forced her hard against his hips. "Lorna hasn't got anything to do with that, and she never will."

"But that's only lust," she whispered desolately.

"That might have been true in the beginning," he agreed. "But there's a lot more to what I feel for you than lust. Dammit, I've loved you all along. It just took me some time to realize that what I felt wasn't going to go away." Wade's eyes were blazing. "And a little more time to own up to it."

His mouth was on hers before she could take another breath, giving and taking, then demanding more as he pressed past the soft barrier of her lips and clashed against her teeth. Magically, they parted beneath the passionate probe of his tongue, and he searched and stroked until she went limp with surrender. Joanna suddenly found herself on the soft coverlet of the bed, trapped partway beneath Wade's hard weight, a jeans-clad leg abrading her silken limbs.

"I want my wife back," he said as he nipped at her love-swollen lips with gentle teeth. "I've waited too damn long as it is for you. Come back to me, Joanna," he said huskily.

"What about Lorna?" she asked while she had some sanity left. "She and Jake are still just friends." Wade withdrew a bit, but didn't release her. "You loved her for so long, you waited for her for so long...."

Wade sighed, his lips slanting in exasperation. "Haven't you been listening, Joanna? I was waiting for the woman I *thought* I was in love with. I found out a few days after I brought you home to the Ten Star that what I felt for her was weakening. I didn't expect to fall for you, but when I did, the intensity of what I felt threw me for a while." Wade's lips moved into a wry smile as he gazed down at her tenderly. "I wasn't prepared to have you come home and turn my feelings upside down. I reckon claiming it was only lust was self-defense," he said, then muttered, "but then that backfired.

"The morning I came over to the Double L after you left me, I began to reap that little lie. I wasn't sure whether to believe you or not when you told me all we'd had was just good sex, and that you felt cheap because of it. You were so damned convincing.

If I hadn't been so stirred up, I would have been able to see that you weren't telling me the truth, either.''

Joanna lay unmoving, too much in awe to speak, too frightened that she might suddenly wake up and discover that this was all a dream. Her heart was bursting with love, and yet fear still hovered there in some small part. Wade had explained a little about her father to her, but she still felt insecure about being loved. She had lived for a long time with what she'd interpreted as rejection.

Wade released a pent-up breath, grumbled something, then eased his length away as he reached toward the night table. Joanna used that opportunity to shift from beneath him, rising to sit in the center of the mattress. She might have put a more rational distance between them while she weighed all he'd just said, if he had not caught her arm and gently forced her to stay.

"Do you feel anything for me at all?" he rasped, apparently having got what he'd been after from the night table. Joanna turned her head and looked over her shoulder at him, gazing helplessly into his eyes as he lay on his side, propped on one forearm. Tears sparkled on her lashes as she searched his face.

Are you going to let the mistakes your old man made with you influence the way you see yourself and how you interpret everyone else's actions for the rest of your life? he'd demanded.

Silently she turned fully toward him. Now was the time to open her heart and take the risk.

"I love you," she whispered at last, feeling a deep,

deep release as the last stronghold of her emotional reserve was breached.

"It's a damned good thing, woman," he growled as he rolled onto his back and pulled her down on top of him. Joanna had started to wind her arms around his neck, when he caught her left hand. "If you'd rather pick out your own rings, just say so. You can have anything you want."

Joanna watched dazedly as he slipped a ruby ring on her finger, and the slim, diamond-studded gold band that was its mate. She stared mutely at the fiery gem and the tiny diamonds that encircled it. Rounded eyes sped up to meet the waiting look in Wade's.

"Is it…are they real?" she stammered, and Wade chuckled softly.

"'Course they are, darlin'," he said with gruff affection.

"I didn't expect—"

"I know you didn't. But I want a real marriage with you. I want everything for us that we didn't have the first three years."

"What about the divorce?" she asked, her heart in her eyes.

"I put a stop to that weeks ago," he said. "In fact, I'd had it stopped the day after our accident, but the papers were mislaid, then delivered to you later by mistake. I don't want to divorce you, Joanna. I just want to love you." Wade hesitated. "Unless you want to go through with it."

"Oh, no. Never," she swore as she slid her hands up his shirtfront. "You're sure?"

Wade rolled toward the center of the bed, swiftly reversing their positions as his mouth came down on hers with a wild ardor that silenced the question and drove it from her mind.

"I love you, Joanna," he rasped when he finally withdrew and hovered over her lips, brushing them softly with his own again and again. "There's no other woman I'll ever want."

"I love you," she echoed urgently, raising her head to try to satisfy the craving that his lips teased from her, as her arms tightened around his lean waist.

The tiny spaghetti strap of her teddy slid off her shoulder, and Wade's eyes caught the movement, his whole body going still as he hooked a finger under the thin string and tugged it slowly downward, uncovering the warm treasure below.

Neither heard the knock at the door, or Lorna's high feminine giggle of delight when it went unanswered. Neither would be aware of anything beyond each other for hours to come.

A LETTER FROM THE AUTHOR

Dear Reader,

It's such a pleasure for me that *Not Part of the Bargain* has been selected for reissue. I'd written it so long ago that even I couldn't remember all the details, so I had to read it again. I was reminded that it is the story of a young woman who had a difficult lonely childhood. Joanna Lloyd Hollister has grown to womanhood with some strong misbeliefs about herself, misbeliefs that impact her adult relationships— particularly her relationship with the man she was forced to marry to cement her father's business deal.

I believe many of us carry a few of the bumps and bruises of our growing-up years, though perhaps not so many as Joanna. *Not Part of the Bargain* is the story of a woman who finally begins to make peace with the events that shaped her, a woman who, by the end of the story, not only gains fresh insight into those events, but also gains a new perspective on herself. Of course, it helps that she also manages to win her husband's heart and make a fresh start toward happily ever after!

I hope you enjoy *Not Part of the Bargain*, whether you're reading it for the first time or, like me, have forgotten enough of the details that you'd like to give it one more read. I hope Joanna's trials and eventual happy ending are an encouragement, and that you will enjoy your visit to the Ten Star.

Hope your life is filled with happily ever afters!

Into the sunset—

Harlequin Romance®

Delightful
Affectionate
Romantic
Emotional

    Tender
    Original

        Daring
        Riveting
        Enchanting
        Adventurous
        Moving

Harlequin Romance®—
capturing the world you dream of...

HARLEQUIN®
Makes any time special ®

HARLEQUIN®
INTRIGUE

WE'LL LEAVE YOU BREATHLESS!

If you've been looking for thrilling tales of
contemporary passion and sensuous love stories
with taut, edge-of-the-seat suspense—then
you'll love Harlequin Intrigue!

Every month, you'll meet four new heroes
who are guaranteed to make your spine tingle
and your pulse pound. With them you'll enter
into the exciting world of Harlequin Intrigue—
where your life is on the line
and so is your heart!

THAT'S INTRIGUE—
ROMANTIC SUSPENSE
AT ITS BEST!

HARLEQUIN®
Makes any time special ®

Harlequin® Historical

*From rugged lawmen and
valiant knights to defiant heiresses
and spirited frontierswomen,
Harlequin Historicals will
capture your imagination with
their dramatic scope, passion
and adventure.*

*Harlequin Historicals . . .
they're too good to miss!*